The Last New York Times
Luis Alejandro Ordóñez

I0682937

Translated by José Ángel Navejas

LUIS ALEJANDRO ORDÓÑEZ

Translated by José Ángel Navejas

The Last
New York Times

katakana
editores

The Last New York Times
First Edition 2019

© Luis Alejandro Ordóñez

© Translated by José Ángel Navejas

Cover picture by Wikimedia Commons. Fernando Pessoa com Costa Brochado no Café Martinho da Arcada, Praça do Comércio, Lisboa. June 6th 1914

Reviewed and corrected by Katelyn O'Brien and Arhur M. Dixon

© Published by katakana editores 2020

Editor: Omar Villasana
Design: Elisa Orozco
Illustrations: Elena Covalciuc Vieriu • @eleart • www.findmyart.com

ISBN: 978-1-7341850-5-8

KATAKANA EDITORES CORP.
Weston FL 33331
✉ katakanaeditores@gmail.com

Table of contents

To Olivia,
the true force behind all my inquiries

whatsoever.

Commiss

for a mee

the matter,

morning, a

owner appe

zoning com

to divide o

Since the

hurricane

tenho de acreditar que é verdade o que eles me dizem,
um jornal não pode mentir, seria o maior pecado do mundo
JOSÉ SARAMAGO, *O Ano da Morte de Ricardo Reis*

New York ~ Cleveland

"Are you done with that?" the passenger in front of him asked.

"No, no..." Benjamin carefully folded the newspaper and began to put it away in the inside pocket of his coat, but the man's questioning look made him think twice, and he tried to offer an explanation.

"It's not today's, it's from a couple of days ago. I'm bringing it to a friend."

The other passenger nodded shortly to let him know he didn't need any more explanations and Benjamin felt certain they wouldn't talk to one another again all the way to Cleveland. It was better that way. Benjamin wasn't in the mood for talking, much less letting someone look at the paper he now guarded so jealously inside his coat.

Benjamin found himself reading the paper now because he hadn't had a chance to look at it before. After each copy was printed, the press assistant had strict orders to destroy the plates. One single reader, one single copy. They couldn't risk printing another. But the paper Benjamin carried with him was left cold, with no reader to be delivered to. Two days before, Benjamin had shown up at his office in the basement of 229 West 43rd Street to find both the undelivered copy and that he no longer had a job.

From the moment he took over *The New York Times*, Hays Sulzberger had been opposed to Benjamin's presence there. Filling his father-in-law's shoes was already difficult enough, and the complaints about Walter Duranty's reports kept coming in, which was why the editor in chief didn't want to run the risk that Benjamin's work might eventually surface. As long as old man Rockefeller remained alive and as long as his son wished to keep him happy, there was very little Hays could do. But as soon as the news of the death of John D. senior got around—and, at *The New York Times*, news travelled fast—a memo was written giving Benjamin a day to vacate his office.

The news had surprised Benjamin—the news of Rockefeller's death, not that he had been fired. The old man had been so confident that he'd live to one hundred that he'd convinced everyone else of it as well. "Three years short," thought Benjamin when he saw the memo, as though deep down he was scolding the old man for not keeping his promise. Shocked and concerned, Benjamin gathered his notes and files, the copy of the newspaper, and a few other belongings. Only the next day did he realize that, for the first time, he was holding in his hands a copy of the paper he had authored himself. That night, unable to sleep, he realized exactly where the final destination of the paper would be, the last one he had written.

So unaccustomed was Benjamin to holding the paper in his hands, it was only the desire to avert his eyes from the view outside the train window that redirected his eyes to the frontpage. In every rundown house, in every abandoned truck or unused road, in every child with torn clothes playing in an empty lot, Benjamin saw the wounds of the unending crisis. He had been lucky, very lucky, first for finding employment at the construction site of the Rockefeller Center towers. Just as construction of one of the first towers was completed, or was about to be completed, Benjamin couldn't really remember, the whole Rockefeller family came to visit the site and old man Rockefeller showed off his sympathy and generosity by handing out coins to anyone who approached him. Even some aldermen and officials got their dimes.

But when, through the strange dynamics of the flow of people, Benjamin and old John D. found themselves face to face, Benjamin refused to accept a coin in exchange for nothing.

"You'll have to buy something from me, sir," said Benjamin to Rockefeller, who was slow to react, somewhat surprised by the young man.

"And what can you offer me?" answered Rockefeller.

Benjamin didn't have to think twice. Of course, he had nothing but a couple of tools, his helmet, and the manuscript of a story he had just finished writing that he was planning on editing during lunch while sitting on a beam of the tower still under construction. He hesitated and then made his decision.

"A story, Mr. Rockefeller. I'm a writer."

Benjamin took the manuscript out from inside the double shirt he wore as protection from the cold winds atop the steel peaks of Manhattan, and he handed it over to the old man.

"It's not signed. What's your name?"

"Benjamin, Benjamin White."

"We're even, Benjamin White," said Rockefeller, handing him the coin and folding the papers so they'd fit inside his coat pocket.

Benjamin never saw Rockefeller again, not even from a distance. He never wrote another story either, although what he wrote for his newspaper counted as just that: fiction.

After gathering his notes and the notebooks in which he kept a record of the stories and news items he wrote, along with the newspaper and a few personal items (a picture of his wife, a pen she'd given him when he landed the job, a copy of *The War of the Worlds* by H.G. Wells, and the coin Rockefeller had given him), Benjamin had no desire to take the train back home. Carrying his small load of mementos, he walked up Seventh Avenue all the way to 50th Street and wondered where the Rockefeller family might be at that moment. Were they on their way to Florida to pick up the body or someplace between where the old man had died and the cemetery where they would bury him? Benjamin recognized a couple of buildings where he had worked, and then he walked up Fifth toward the park. He stayed there until darkness compelled him to leave.

Back home, his wife was waiting for him, worried not so much about how late it was but about how his emotional state might be. When he got home that Sunday and realized his wife hadn't heard the news, he decided to keep it to himself. Benjamin left for work on Monday as if nothing had happened, partly in denial, partly expecting that either the newspaper or the foundation would offer him good news regarding his fate in either organization. A couple of hours later, Susan finally found out from a conversation with the neighbors after mass. She wanted to go look for Benjamin, but she also knew the best thing to do was to wait in silence, like a good wife, like the good wife she had turned out to be when her husband told her he'd changed jobs, he'd left construction for a strange position between the Rockefeller Foundation and *The New York Times*. Susan never understood her husband's job, she didn't understand the reason why Mr. Rockefeller, the son, wanted his father to read fake news; it's deceitful, lying to one's own father, it's got to be a sin; Susan swallowed her thoughts and harbored a somewhat guilty silence. After all, Benjamin was part of that sin.

Susan had not lacked for anything since she'd married Benjamin, during times when simply having enough to eat was reason enough to be eternally grateful, but now they'd been married almost five years and they still hadn't been blessed with a child, which was what Susan wanted most in life. Since Benjamin had started working in such a reprehensible occupation, Susan feared that their inability to conceive might be divine punishment, and she prayed and asked for forgiveness every day for the lies Benjamin would have to write.

When she heard from her husband that, indeed, with the old man dead there would be no more paper to write, she felt relieved and hoped God would forgive her. The next day, Benjamin was going to try to go back to his old construction job at Rockefeller Center, where a few buildings still needed to be finished, but after staying up too late and the turbulent emotions of the past two days, Benjamin slept in past noon. He accompanied Susan to church where they prayed. She prayed, like every day, to make amends for her husband's sins, and he prayed for the future, which seemed utterly uncertain.

Benjamin thought he wasn't the same person anymore, he couldn't go back to work in the skyscrapers. It wasn't easy, climbing up on a beam 100 feet above the ground and hammering and screwing and fighting vertigo, fighting against the wind and the cold. It wasn't that he had become softer, as his job at the newspaper wasn't any less difficult—writing four full pages every day, eight on Fridays so the Saturday edition would be ready and he could take the day off and start again on Sunday. But going back to work in construction would mean giving up, losing what little prestige he had earned through his written work, and why shouldn't he call it that, three straight years writing and publishing, even if it had only been for one single reader and the proofs had been destroyed afterward. He knew the paper existed and he wrote it, he had gained experience, he was capable of turning any event that happened in the world into a beautiful story of hope, he knew when an event deserved only brief mention or when it was worth writing about in several parts, developing the story to its conclusion. Whoever happened to read the paper, if an occasional copy was left behind in one of the Rockefeller residences, would certainly think so; that was how the old man saw it, or at least that was what Benjamin concluded, since no one ever said otherwise or complained to him about inappropriate content or about a disheartening or unbelievable story, and above all because only the old man's death had put an end to his work.

None of that was any use now. His notebooks were nothing more than that, notes. Nobody at *The New York Times* would vouch that he was part of their team because he wasn't, and nobody at the Rockefeller Foundation knew him, except perhaps some accountant in charge of recording his weekly wages. The only proof of his work during the last three years was the copy of the newspaper that had been left unread and that he had picked up from his desk.

He didn't want to read the paper. Not the last one. Not the one he had ended up with because no one knew what to do with it. Benjamin took this as a sign of respect, but he couldn't fool himself—that copy was not meant for him. Somewhere in the halls of the Times Square Building, someone certainly knew who he was, even though they were careful not to say anything to him. Perhaps the very fact that they were so careful was tacit proof that they knew what he did. The newspaper of old man Rockefeller, only read by the powerful, venerable old gentleman himself. When no one came to get it, they decided to just leave it there. Benjamin would not be the only one to violate the fear and respect generated by that mysterious newspaper that had once embarked every day to wherever John D. Rockefeller happened to be.

When he woke up on Tuesday, he told his wife he was going to the old man's funeral, and he'd think about the future after that. She remained silent, as she usually did whenever her husband mentioned anything related to his job at the newspaper, or whenever he spoke about the future.

After going to mass with his wife, he set out to find out where the funeral would be; it didn't take him long. The news was a hot item, and *The New York Times* itself, the one with the real news, announced that the burial would take place on Thursday at Lake View cemetery in Cleveland, where the family already had an obelisk in homage to their kin buried there.

After having wasted most of the day sleeping, Benjamin decided it was probably better to take the rest of Tuesday for himself and leave as early as possible for Grand Central the next morning. With a suitcase containing only his best Sunday suit, which he'd wear at the funeral, he boarded the train for Cleveland.

Traveling by train always gave Benjamin a strange sensation, as though he suddenly found himself in a strange, unknown reality. Through the window, he saw houses, trees, fields, buildings passing by, but it all seemed fake, like models in a museum exhibit. He wondered how things might look from up in the air, from an airship, for instance, and he remembered that only a few weeks before he had included the successful transatlantic voyage of the Hindenburg in the newspaper. It was rare for him to do this: take a certain event, a tragedy like that of the Hindenburg, and recount it with a happy ending. He considered it an important risk. It was almost certain that many people, important people, people who travelled the world, visited Rockefeller. During those conversations someone could make a comment about current events, did you hear about the Hindenburg airship, Mr. Rockefeller, yes, what a beautiful flight, I wish I could have been there. No, it was one thing to keep the old man happy, quite another to make people start treating him as though he were senile.

But in the picture unfolding before him through the train window, Benjamin recognized many stories of his own invention. Stories from Rockefeller's paper that had told of people overcoming the aftermath of the Great Depression with spunk and determination suddenly appeared through the window, demanding that Benjamin provide an errata sheet. It was better to find shelter in the ever pleasant pages of *The New York Times* that he carried on his lap.

Reading himself in the newspaper for the first time was a complete revelation. Such a curious thing—to recognize each and every article, each and every sentence, each and every word, but at the same time to feel like they were so foreign to him, as though they didn't belong to him because, in fact, they didn't. He found a somewhat unclear sentence, a misused adjective, two switched letters, and there was nothing he could do about it. Had there been a reader, he would have had to decipher what Benjamin meant to say with that sentence, contrasting the adjective with his own knowledge of its true meaning, and shifting the letters as though he were dyslexic. Being able to open his newspaper, flip through the pages, read each story, each op-ed, each article was a completely unexpected pleasure, a pleasure *The New York Times* had robbed him of for fear that the newspaper would make its way beyond John D. Rockefeller's surroundings. The old man wanted his own newspaper, with personalized news items tailored to his liking, why was it such a bad thing for others to read them as well? They didn't even allow Benjamin to keep copies for his personal records. After three years of writing the newspaper the old man read every morning, Benjamin had kept only the last issue because that day, May 24th, there was no longer anyone to deliver it to.

While working on the May 24th edition, Benjamin received the news of John D. Rockefeller's death at 97 years of age and, consistent with his role at the paper, he set that item aside as one that could not be included in the day's edition. He finished his work, which consisted of four pages, turned the plates in, and left for the day. The next day, the last edition of *The New York Times*, the one that did not include the news of John D. Rockefeller's death in order to avoid any risk that the old man would read it, was waiting for him right next to the memo ordering him to vacate the office by the next day at the latest.

He was never truly sure how the mechanism worked. Who he answered to. Who gave him orders or who paid him. The envelope of money always arrived punctually on his desk, the same way that the newspaper arrived punctually in the hands of John

Sr., he imagined. But at *The New York Times* they ignored him completely, and he never had to report to the offices of the Rockefeller Foundation, if it was indeed the foundation that was responsible for overseeing his job; perhaps his payment came directly from Standard Oil itself. What was certain was that the contempt he felt from the *Times* and his distance from the Foundation and the oil company gave Benjamin the liberty to create his newspaper like a true work of art every day—something singular, original, unique, and impossible to replicate.

The secret lay in his method. Benjamin started by reading the *Times*, and from there he chose his stories. He also kept notes of what he heard on the street, on the train, in conversations with friends, so he could incorporate stories of everyday people. Once he decided on the topics, he chose the titles and started writing them all at once because he had no time to waste turning things over in his head. The easiest news, like that of the successful flight of the Hindenburg, he saved for last. The most difficult ones were the others, the ones that demanded he recreate lives and personal stories, adverse circumstances overcome through persistence, or altruistic spirits who helped out others from their privileged social positions or from wherever they found themselves by chance. A central aspect of his credibility was never repeating himself, even if the stories he wrote were similar. The worst thing that could happen to Rockefeller's *New York Times* would be for the old man to think that a particular news item he was reading could not be true.

Arriving at Union Terminal in Cleveland, Benjamin asked whether it was easy to get to the cemetery from there. It would be a long walk along Euclid Avenue, but when Benjamin told the attendant at the station he had plenty of time, since he didn't have to be at the cemetery until the next day, the attendant answered that he was lucky because along Euclid Avenue were many mansions that had been converted into guesthouses.

In fact, many wealthy families had once lived along that avenue, but most of the houses now were either abandoned or had been converted into guesthouses. Benjamin assumed the area had been hit hard by the Great Depression, but he also imagined he could say the same about any other place in the country he might visit. Once again, he felt grateful for his good luck and then regretted that it was about to change, possibly for the worse. He wanted to resist that idea; he wanted to think that he could show up at a newspaper, maybe right there in Cleveland, and get a job. There were many stories to tell, true stories, the war in Spain and the situation in Europe, the struggle to overcome the Depression itself, and who knows what else. And he had the penmanship, the experience—someone somewhere would surely be interested in giving him a new opportunity. All he needed to do was find that person.

Benjamin found a room in one of the old mansions. The housekeeper told him he was lucky; in two days he wouldn't have been able to find a vacancy.

"Why?" asked Benjamin, somewhat confused.

"The Great Lakes Exposition starts on the 29th. Last year it was a great success. This year we expect even more people to come."

"And what's in the exposition?"

"All sorts of things—music, food, industry pavilions, even a farm. The first exposition was most interesting, good fun. People came for several days, most of them for entertainment, but some were looking for jobs or doing business. Cleveland had almost never seen anything like it."

"Interesting. Maybe I'll stick around a little longer so I can check it out."

"How long are you planning on staying?"

"At first I was thinking I'd go back to New York on Friday, but the exposition sounds like something I'd be interested in. There should be journalists and businessmen there. It would be a good place to make some contacts."

"And what brought you to Cleveland, if you don't mind my asking?"

"I came for the Rockefeller funeral. I'd like to pay my respects."

"Did you know him?"

"We spoke once, and I worked for him indirectly."

"The Rockefeller family lived on this very street a long time ago."

"Really?"

"Those were different times. Nobody wants to remember that this used to be called Millionaire's Row."

"You can see the past in the houses."

"But that's all."

Benjamin realized that the conversation had reached an uncomfortable point for the housekeeper. Who knew if she herself had once been the lady of the house with a dozen employees at her service. Not saying another word, Benjamin took the key to his room and made his way upstairs.

"It's the third door," said the housekeeper from below.

Judging by the size, the quality of the woodwork, and the details in the columns, it was plain to see that these were the remains of an age of abundance. But, judging by the bareness of the walls and the shabbiness of the furniture, everything of any value had been taken from the house, perhaps to sell, perhaps to protect from the guests, perhaps stolen. All the speculations he could make about the house, the housekeeper, and the neighbors were just that, simple speculations, but they still had the potential to harm him. This trip was beginning to fill Benjamin with great sadness. Not that he regretted taking it, it was simply that reality was sending him too many messages, as if dedicating himself to writing the paper had pushed him into living a little too long in the fantasy world that he had created every day in its pages. He didn't know he was so vulnerable, not until he took the train to Cleveland.

Benjamin was tired. He went to bed early and slept deeply, even though the bed was uncomfortable and the blanket was not warm enough for the spring Cleveland night. But he didn't think much, at least not about the future, and that was good enough.

Upon waking, Benjamin put on his Sunday best and left for the cemetery. He knew the ceremony would be private, but he was planning to stand there holding out the copy of *The New York Times* while the procession went by to see if John Jr. or one of his assistants would recognize him. It had been John Jr. who had shown up at the construction site a couple of days after the encounter between his father and Benjamin. The heir of the Rockefeller empire told him that since his father had stopped playing golf very few things had made him as happy as the story Benjamin had given him.

"My father said that's how newspapers should be," John Jr. told Benjamin. "He said he wished *The New York Times* were like that. That's when I had the idea."

After that, John did nothing but thank Benjamin and take his leave. The whole plan, the agreement with *The New York Times*, Benjamin's role and pay, were explained to him by the heir's assistants.

Yes, Benjamin knew his plan to be a part of old man Rockefeller's funeral procession and burial might not work, but he truly desired to leave the last issue of the newspaper at his grave. If he didn't succeed in joining them, he'd wait for the funeral to end and then have his own little ceremony. After all, it had always been just him and old Rockefeller.

But apparently this time it wouldn't be so. As soon as he arrived at the entrance to the cemetery, Benjamin realized he'd be just one more face in a crowd of curious onlookers who wanted to see the funeral procession go by, whether to bid farewell to the millionaire, the man who had not been born in Cleveland but who grew up there and started his empire there, or simply to gawk at important people, as occasions like these are very rare in a city like this one, a city of factories and industries that had collapsed after the Depression.

Benjamin tried to enter the cemetery, but the security guard stopped him at the door. No access was allowed until after the private ceremony. He went back to join the crowd of curious onlookers and stood by the driveway ready to hold out the copy of Rockefeller's *New York Times* and show it to the family as they passed by.

But the coffin went by and so did every one of his relatives, and not one of them stopped in front of Benjamin and the out-stretched paper. Many of the onlookers dispersed. Others, includ-ing Benjamin, waited for the ceremony to end. Maybe once the funeral was over some of the celebrities would be willing to ex-change a few words with them. When the family began to leave, more scattered now than when they had gone in, Benjamin took up his position again, and again no one stopped to look at him.

The last few cars, which Benjamin assumed contained John D. Junior and his family, drove away. Behind them followed the last of the onlookers and, about ten minutes later, the doors of the cemetery were opened again. Benjamin asked if there would be a problem if he visited the tomb and the security guard an-swered no.

Benjamin walked in the direction of the gravesite, which was easy to spot thanks to the obelisk that towered over the lawn. The old man's grave was set between his wife's and mother's. Benja-min approached it and left the copy of *The New York Times* that had never reached Rockefeller in life on top of some floral ar-rangements. Then, without fully knowing whether for the old man or for himself, he began to cry.

There was nothing left to do there. That was the end. The pa-per he had left over Rockefeller's grave was the last edition of *The New York Times*, of his paper, *The New York Times* that was as much his as it was the old man's. Rockefeller had wanted to read what he wanted, and when he had the paper in front of him he read it the same way he always had, he read it according to who he was, but Benjamin always wrote what he could and, in order to do his best, he had to transform himself, to look at the world in a different way, develop new voices, rise to the level of something he didn't know, something he'd never known before, Rockefeller, that entelechy, that person who remained unknown despite his fame, who sat reading his special paper every day. Benjamin had to know what he read, what news he slowed down for, which stories he skipped, which ones he read over and over, which ones bored him to death, which ones he disliked but kept reading. Benjamin never knew any of this, so he kept writing, writing as though he himself were Rockefeller, as if he were an old multimillionaire who gave away most of his fortune to charity because what was left was enough, was too much, too much for anyone else, too much for Benjamin who thanks to the newspaper lived comfortably but didn't have any more than necessary. How could he put himself in the shoes of someone who could give everything away so lavishly because he would never be in need? And yet that was what Benjamin did, what he tried to do for more than three years. Who knows whether he achieved it or not. The only one who could judge was right there, lying at his feet, forever silent.

As soon as he left the cemetery, regret almost made him go back. He had just left behind the only proof of his existence for the last three years. Now that he thought about it, the fact that the paper ended up in his hands was a mistake. Old man Rockefeller's death and the end of Benjamin's employment had caused the guardians of the journalistic prestige of *The New York Times* to lower their guard, and a single copy, which was evidence enough, had slipped through their fingers. Perhaps in a few days they would show up at his apartment asking what he had done with the last issue, demanding proof that he had in fact left it at Rockefeller's grave. Perhaps they had already been there and Susan had only been able to tell them that her husband was in Cleveland. Maybe upon hearing this confession the gentlemen, Hays's go-betweens, had surmised Benjamin's intentions. But deep down Benjamin knew, most likely, no one had wondered about the last copy. It was a three-day-old issue, who would be interested in it? All newspapers becomes somehow fictitious as the days go by. The news stops making sense because of the oblivion that subjugates both facts and men. With time, the paper Benjamin wrote for Rockefeller would become exactly equal to and completely indistinguishable from any other issue of the true *The New York Times*. That was why no one had knocked at the door and no one would. That copy of *The New York Times* was only important for him. It only had meaning for him—he was the only one who could, and should, keep it. And the only thing that had occurred to Benjamin was to leave it as an offering at a gravesite where, within a day or two at most, the wind, the rain, or the maintenance staff would destroy it forever. Even though he knew that without the newspaper it would be hard for him to convince anyone he had written a fake version of *The New York Times* for three years, Benjamin didn't go back for it. If his life during the following years became some sort of fiction, it would be the result of a job well done. He was the main fiction told between the lines of the fake edition's pages. Now it was a matter of closing the cycle and paying homage. Still doubtful, Benjamin continued walking until he became as decisive as he had been when he stood with the outstretched paper watching the funeral procession go by.

Benjamin went back to the guesthouse without knowing what to do. He was tired and wanted to sleep. In the last three days he really hadn't done much, not like he used to, and even still, he felt constantly tired, sleepy; it was best to fight against it. He asked the housekeeper whether she had anything he could write on, and she gave him the best thing she could find: a couple of pages from a notebook where she kept her daily records and guest payments, as well as a piece of charcoal that some artist or aspiring artist had once left in the bedroom and that had ended up in the house-keeper's desk. Benjamin felt tempted to ask her about her back-ground: Had she been part of the mansion's glory days or did she arrive there later, when decay had already settled into the rooms like a guest of honor, or like a visitor who isn't wanted but is im-possible to kick out? But Benjamin realized he couldn't stay there if the housekeeper started to speak, he wouldn't be able to toler-ate it, as if the absence of the newspaper had also robbed him of the meaning in listening to such stories.

Once in his room, with paper and charcoal ready, Benjamin thought for a while about what he felt in the presence of the house-keeper. Suddenly, the idea of not being able to control the world seemed terrible to him. Maybe that was exactly what Rockefel-ler felt.

In the silence of the guesthouse, the first story, the one that had cost the old man 10 cents, came back to him. The story was not similar to the newspaper. It was a love story with a happy ending, but it only spoke of the tribulations of lovers, without any social context or any reference to personal growth beyond that of the couple, who lived happily ever after. Why had Rocke-feller liked it? Why did John D. Jr.'s assistants instruct Benjamin to write a paper filled with good news? Maybe the old man real-ly had said that's how newspapers ought to be, filled with good news only. He spent hours thinking about these things and the invincible sleep from days past overcame him. The paper and charcoal ended up on the floor, unused.

He woke up early, still undecided about whether to stay a cou-ple more days or return to New York that very afternoon. On the way downstairs, however, he had to make a quick decision. The housekeeper was waiting to ask him whether she could of-fer the room to the people who were starting to arrive for the

Exposition. Seeing that, in fact, there were several people, even an entire family (father, mother, two boys, and a girl), waiting their turn, Benjamin thought it might be worthwhile to check out the event. Businessmen, people from different industries, journalists, people with connections, who knows who could be there, so why not stay. After confirming that he'd stay until Monday morning, he left the guesthouse to look for a telegraph office where he could write his wife. "Coming back Monday. Looking for business this weekend."

The Exposition would start the following day, so he had a long Friday ahead of him with nothing to do. He asked the person in charge of writing the telegrams about the Indians and she confirmed that they were in the city.

"It's a shame today is Friday. You'll have to go to the old park. They use the new one on Sundays, especially during the summer."

"Do you follow them closely?"

"No, but I work at the telegraph, so I need to know about everything."

"And do you know who they're playing today?"

"The White Sox."

Benjamin was sorry they weren't playing against the Yankees. It would've been fun to have the chance to insult Gehrig, DiMaggio, Gomez, and company in a different city. He was a Giants fan, having grown up near and still living very close to the Polo Grounds. As a result, he didn't know much about the teams in the American League, except for the despised Yankees. To watch a game between the Indians and the White Sox would be to witness the purity of the game again, to appreciate the shape of the ball because it was beautiful, without having to agonize over the final score, be it a defeat or a victory, because sometimes you wish for a victory so much, you become part of it so much, that it hurts just as much, it feels like losing.

He went back to the guesthouse to clean up a little and left again for the stadium. He ate lunch close to the ballpark and bought his ticket. The White Sox defeated the Indians 3 to 2 in 10 innings.

After the game, without realizing it, Benjamin continued his homage as he roamed through the city and ended up at Rockefeller Park, one of the gifts the millionaire had given to the city. Benjamin again thought it wasn't clear to him why he was still in Cleveland. Quite frankly, he didn't know why he had gone there to begin with. Leaving the paper at the gravesite was an impulse, an empty tribute to someone who didn't truly need it. What did the old man really need? Nothing. To wait. To wait for death, or to wait until he turned 100, which as a goal is nothing more than a way of masking the fact that the only thing left in life is waiting for death. Benjamin's paper helped the old man out during his wait, masking reality for unknown reasons. The fact that it was good news didn't remove the certainty of the end, and the effort was merely an attempt to brighten the old man's monotonous days, not to make him feel immortal.

Only when he used to talk to Susan about his day at the newspaper had he felt overwhelmed by the senselessness of his work the way he felt now. But in front of his wife he tried not to reflect on the old man's motives, or his son's, but instead to appease the many fears that his job elicited in Susan. Walking past the garden, Benjamin understood it all, or at least he wanted to believe he did. He had merely been another of the old man's charity projects. The very last one. Rockefeller never had any desire to read good news. The news was Benjamin himself, who went from construction worker to editor in chief at *The New York Times* with one single stroke of a pen. That's why the story that Rockefeller read had nothing to do with the task Benjamin was given, that's why the whole deal bothered everyone at *The New York Times* so much, that's why nobody recognized him or the newspaper at the funeral. Benjamin mattered little in all of this, what was important was that an old man felt satisfied each morning thanks to the paper he received punctually that told him on each and every one of its pages and lines that yes, his experiment had worked and, with that, all his other experiments as well, yes, it was possible to change a person's life, and Benjamin reminded the old man of that until his last day. Rockefeller died in peace thanks to Benjamin's effort.

Now, for the first time in three years, Benjamin was alone without the strange benefactor who had created a job for him just so he could surprise him.

He went back to the guesthouse and into his room. The paper and charcoal were there. It was a beginning, a very small beginning, but it would be enough for today. The next day a new paper would be published. ⌗

561-615-195

561-27-195

DCF

legislati

 have no

ain catego

licensu

18

Lisbon

ven if the differences between the two places were insignif-
icant, the error in the photograph's caption showed the mag-
nitude of his failure. It was not Daytona Beach, it was Ormond
Beach, and even though Gilberto had never been to the United
States and didn't have a clear idea of what Florida beaches might
be like, for him it was a matter of honor knowing that John D.
Rockefeller once had a summer house in Ormond Beach and not
Daytona Beach, and that it was there that he died.

The *Diário de Lisboa* dedicated only a single picture in the lower right corner of the page to Rockefeller's death and, as if that
wasn't enough, they made a mistake: "The last picture of John
Rockefeller, 'the King of Oil,' who died yesterday at 97 years of age
at his winter home in Daytona Beach, Florida."

At least the picture was big enough to show the old man in all
his glory. The man who wanted to live 100 years and who gave almost all of his fortune to charity. Such poor taste, better not to
mention that and instead characterize him only as the "King of
Oil." Gilberto was not satisfied at all with such meager coverage,
but he couldn't expect otherwise. During the past year, he had
dedicated special attention to the figure of the tycoon, but he had
never managed to pass on his enthusiasm to the newspaper's
director. This caption was the final message his boss had sent
him. And by final, Gilberto meant just that, final. Before heading to the Bragança Hotel, he stopped by the telegraph office
and sent a short message: "Saturday last day. I quit."

In a few years telegraphs will be able to send pictures, thought Gilberto with sad irony. His telegram was missing the force of an image letting Mr. Manso know he had taken the brief coverage as a personal affront. But what did Gilberto know about the future? He hadn't thought about the future when he walked into the telegraph office and dictated his resignation. He only asked himself "and now what?" after the message had been sent, not by wire, because the distance was so short, but right inside the mailman's bag. The person in charge of the telegraph even told him he could deliver the message himself and save an escudo, but Gilberto didn't want to set foot in 44 Luz Soriano Street ever again.

In the dining room of the Bragança he wondered whether being so decisive had been worth it. He hadn't been especially keen on the story, at least not at first. Afterward, with the director's continuous rejection, the matter became more and more personal, and this ending seemed like the logical evolution of the situation. Rockefeller died when he wasn't on duty. They could have contacted him to write something, nothing too much—after all, the *Diário de Lisboa* was an evening paper and by Monday afternoon the news would be considered old, but still, that didn't explain the photo caption. Again, anger swept over Gilberto and again he was convinced that he had no other choice but to quit.

The first time he heard about Rockefeller's good newspaper was from his sister, who was ten years older than him. It was a day when news from neighboring Spain regarding imminent conflict made the members of the Gomes family, who usually met for a long lunch after Sunday mass, particularly pessimistic. There, between prewar reports and questions of what-will-become-of-us, Maria said it was their fault for reading so many papers. "The newspapers lie," Gilberto remembered his sister saying, before adding that this was the reason why kings and millionaires had their own papers written for them. Up to then, it had seemed like a generic comment. Actually, Gilberto thought, millionaires could buy entire newspapers to either lie or tell uncomfortable truths, but this thought was interrupted by what Maria said next: "Like old man Rockefeller, who gets a newspaper with nothing but good news in it, because that's what he likes to read."

Family gatherings are always disorderly and loud, ideas come and go, and feelings as well, and the topics change rapidly, moving from disagreement to oblivion, leaving no trace, no wounds, no grudges. Some comment took the conversation in a different direction and neither Rockefeller nor the veracity of the paper was mentioned again that afternoon. Gilberto forgot about the story until it came back to him, as should be expected, in an unexpected way.

An old friend from college, the poet Paulo Salcido, was waiting for him in front of his house with the day's edition of the *Diário de Lisboa*, ready to reproach him, but he decided to contain himself until lunch.

"Do you want to go to the Bragança Hotel? The food there is very good."

"Which of the two?"

"The one on Alecrim Street. It's not too far from the newspaper office."

Gilberto used to start work after lunch, and he would sometimes stay at the office until after midnight, when the new issue was almost ready, or at least the stories or pages he was responsible for. The sports section was still not that important in the paper, which is why its length or place would often change; sometimes Gilberto had a double page at his disposal, and sometimes it was not even half a page.

When he met with Paulo, their conversations always started with sports, which the poet deeply hated. However, Gilberto never knew whether it was out of sarcasm or genuine curiosity that his friend always asked him about the Benfica or the car races. At any rate, Gilberto would always bring him up to date.

But on that occasion the poet went directly to the point and, before they ordered, Paulo was already complaining to him about the meager space the paper had dedicated to the death of the great poet Fernando Pessoa, especially considering that Pessoa had been a long-time contributor to the paper. Gilberto tried to defend himself: it wasn't his section, Pessoa had died on Sunday and it was already Tuesday, giving him so much space wouldn't have made sense.

"Yes, it would have. I'm telling you, Pessoa's importance will get bigger with time, and this brief note will remain there as a document," said Paulo as he handed the copy of the *Diário* to Gilberto.

Gilberto read the note and couldn't help but ask the poet what else could have been added.

"The heteronyms, for instance. Not only one poet died—at least four died, who knows how many more!"

Paulo had to explain to Gilberto what a heteronym was, the same way that Pessoa himself had in his *Biographic Table*, but it was a comparison in the explanation that really stuck with Gilberto:

"They're not just pseudonyms—rather, if you can forgive the childish comparison, they're more like Rockefeller's *New York Times*. It's the same paper with different topics, with different news, with a different personality. For instance, if it had the name *The Rockefeller Times*, it would be a completely different paper from *The New York Times*."

"Rockefeller's *New York Times*?"

"The tycoon has his own personal version of *The New York Times* made with nothing but good news in it, because apparently he doesn't like the world the way it is."

Gilberto didn't pay much attention to the rest of what Paulo told him about Pessoa. The idea of a personal newspaper written for a millionaire seemed as interesting to him as it had when he'd first heard it at home from his sister. Last time, he'd simply forgotten the story; this time he wouldn't.

That very afternoon, he proposed the idea to the director of the newspaper. Mr. Manso didn't see much of a story nor was he too interested in Gilberto's idea. Visibly disappointed, Gilberto went to his desk to see what material he had to work with for the sports section. There was a boxing match, scores from the Spanish soccer league and a complaint about a game between Sporting and Carcavelinhos, which would apparently be settled at a referee meeting. It only took a couple of calls to obtain the information he needed, including the upgrades to the Belenenses stadium. Depending on the space they gave him, he almost had the section ready. After all, as it was Tuesday, he didn't expect more than a column, half a page at the most.

He was waiting for instructions and already writing a bit about the Sporting game conflict when Mr. Manso approached him and asked him what aspect of Rockefeller's story had caught his interest.

Gilberto was not expecting the newspaper director to approach him so suddenly and, besides thinking it seemed like a story worth pursuing, he hadn't really thought through his interest in it.

"I don't know. It seemed important. He's a millionaire who can have his own newspaper. The truth is, I thought there was a story there."

That was not what Manso wanted to hear. He had always believed in Gilberto, even when the young man insisted on writing only about sports, which the director saw as a sign of laziness. "In sports the stories come ready-made," he said once, watching to see Gilberto's reaction. But nothing moved him, nothing interested him, and just when Gilberto came to him with a different story, with a topic that could be interesting, Manso was distracted; he was too busy to spot the chance to be a mentor. When he finished two different things he was working on, he realized he'd missed an opportunity. He still thought the story was nonsense, unfounded gossip, but he wanted to give Gilberto a chance. Manso would've liked to see a passionate Gilberto, someone interested in telling the story, in creating it and presenting it to the world, but the young man showed his true colors again, as usual, a bureaucrat who just happened to be there the same way he could have been in any other office in the city.

"Son, there is no story without a father," Mr. Manso said to Gilberto. He added, before heading back to his office, "We have pictures of the boxing match. Write something longer about it."

The article was about the boxing matches the next day, featuring welterweight Portuguese champion Horacio Velha, who would face a French boxer named Oscar Degieux, and a powerful Brazilian boxer named Brasilino Fino who would also face a Frenchman, Albert Lepesant. When he finished the article, Gilberto had to fill some space in the column they had given him for the sports section, since the boxing article would appear on a different page, next to an article on music. It was not until he made sure both pages were ready that he thought again about what Mr. Manso had said to him.

Walking home late at night, Gilberto became convinced that the director was inviting him to insist on the Rockefeller story. For the first time in his career, he took the time to reflect on and even plan what he'd have to do to land an article. He'd have to do more research, find a contact at *The New York Times*, or maybe get a copy of the paper and then speak directly to the millionaire or to someone in the family who could explain why they had to have a special paper made to order. "Why not?" Gilberto would answer if he were Rockefeller. When you have as many millions to give away as the old man, "why not" is the answer to every whim. Every decision, every project becomes utterly whimsical with Rockefeller's millions. That's the story, not Rockefeller's newspaper. That was the last thought to cross Gilberto's mind before he went to bed.

The next day, Gilberto got up and left a little earlier than usual. He went toward Chiado so he could stop by the Bertrand bookstore. That was a good place to start because, even if he couldn't find *The New York Times* there, they could probably give him a hint about where to find some copies.

But at the bookstore they told him the best thing to do was to ask among journalists. The foreign papers they had were all European. The United States was far away and a newspaper from there wouldn't arrive until many days after it was published, which from a business perspective didn't make much sense.

Thus, his best chance would probably be Mr. Manso himself. For the second day in a row, the first thing Gilberto did upon arriving at the offices of the *Diário de Lisboa* was knock on the director's door.

This time Mr. Manso was ready to give Gilberto all the attention he needed.

"I've been thinking about what you said and about Rockefeller's story. I think it would be interesting to look for one of those issues, see what kind of news it has and ask Mr. Rockefeller why he has his own paper written that way."

Manso looked at Gilberto for a moment and perceived a genuine interest.

"And where would you like to start?"

"I'd like to see a copy of *The New York Times*. I've never seen one, I don't know what kind of paper we're talking about. That's why I wanted to see you, I wanted to ask you if you happen to have a copy."

He did have one. Every once in a while friends and contacts who had recently come back from the US brought him copies that he stowed away, partly out of professional interest and partly as a collector's hobby. He had copies of papers from all over the world. He looked through his stockpile and found the most recent issue he had of *The New York Times*. He handed it to Gilberto who leafed through it quickly.

"Difficult, isn't it?" said Mr. Manso, but Gilberto didn't understand what he meant and the director stopped talking. "Take it with you, but don't take it out of the office and don't forget that there's boxing today."

Gilberto didn't have anything to do that afternoon, since the only space he had to fill the following day was related to the boxing matches, which meant he'd have to write it at night. The copy of *The New York Times* the director had lent him was from Sunday, November 10, and even though Gilberto didn't know English, he was able to make out the sports scores on the first page. He was impressed by the size of the paper's sports section. He fancied his own version of *The New York Times*, with a whole page dedicated to Benfica, another one to Sporting, a whole section full of photos and scores from Portuguese soccer, another one dedicated to the next Olympic Games in Berlin. Yes, an American newspaper could do it, a millionaire like Rockefeller could do it, and even though Gilberto had no clue about business, he suddenly wished he could turn into a Rockefeller himself, so he could have his own personalized version of *The New York Times*.

Gilberto left, heading out to a café or park to kill the rest of the evening before the boxing match, which would take place about ten minutes away from the newspaper offices, at the Dos Recreios Coliseum.

When it was almost time to go to the coliseum, he saw Paulo walking toward him, but he passed by him hurriedly.

"Poet! Where are you going in such a hurry?"

"It's match night."

"I'm going too, I have to cover it for the paper."

"I can finally see the advantage of working on sports news, going to boxing matches without having to find an excuse."

"But what's your excuse? I thought you didn't like sports."

"I don't like sports, but boxing is different, it's two men fighting to stay on their feet, it's civilization against barbarism."

"And how do you know which one of the two boxers is the civilized one?"

"It's not the boxers, it's the ropes, the bell, the referee. Civilization is found at the limits."

For a moment Gilberto thought he might talk about that in his article, but he decided not to get too philosophical and to start by noting the growing popularity of boxing, a sport on the rise, no doubt, in which the fighters had become true celebrities.

Brasilino defeated the French fighter by default, while Velha, the champion, knocked down the other Frenchman in the fifth round. In the other fight of the night, Salvador Prospero, the Spaniard, defeated Portugal's own Joao Quintino. The night went by quickly and none of the matches lasted more than seven rounds, which made it hard for Gilberto to turn down the poet, who kept insisting on taking him out for a drink.

"I have to write this article, it has to go out tomorrow. But we can meet tomorrow evening, I have the day off because I worked late today. I have a favor to ask you."

They parted ways and agreed to meet at the Bertrand bookstore, which Gilberto deemed an appropriate place for the favor he wanted to ask his friend.

"Do you know English?" Gilberto asked the poet as soon as they met.

"A little."

"I need a favor, I want to write a letter to *The New York Times*."

"Sure. Tell me what it's about and I'll do my best."

Gilberto told him he was trying to find out about Rockefeller's *New York Times*, and he was writing to the newspaper to see whether they could send him a copy of it. Paulo liked the idea and suggested they should also write the Rockefeller family, who might have copies of it as well. Paulo volunteered to find the family's mailing address and Gilberto gave him the address for

The New York Times that he had copied from the issue Mr. Manso had lent him.

It then became a matter of waiting for an answer from *The New York Times* or the Rockefeller family, leaving Gilberto with only one tool with which to write his article: patience. Who knows what routes letters must travel to reach their destination. They left the post office for the port; they got on a boat headed for America. Did the ship go straight to the States or did it stop at some island? Did it pass through the Azores or through Madeira? And, arriving in the US, did it dock in Boston, Baltimore, or New York? From there, did the letters continue by ship or by train? Someday there will be a more direct system, thought Gilberto, but today there's only a very slight possibility that the letters will travel on one single ship from Lisbon to New York. And after that, what will it be like at the office where the mail gets distributed at the headquarters of *The New York Times*? How do they handle the mail for the Rockefeller family? If the letters reach their destination, the most important question still remains: Will they answer the request? After all, the easiest thing would be to ignore the letter altogether. That's why waiting didn't make any sense. It was better to forget about the whole thing and then pretend to be surprised. One day, the mailman will knock at the door and give him an envelope with a copy of *The New York Times*, almost as though he were John D. Rockefeller himself, oil tycoon, millionaire philanthropist who has his own paper made with the news that he wants, because in the end it seems money can indeed buy everything, even reality.

It was in April of the following year. The sender of the package was the Rockefeller Foundation itself, without any other kind of identification, as though the Foundation were a person. The excitement he felt when he saw the word "Rockefeller" and his own surname written on the same envelope was beyond anything that he had ever experienced before and could probably only be compared with seeing his name alongside a newspaper article, since in the *Diário de Lisboa* only a few specific types of articles featured the author's name. But the excitement was a necessary preamble to the utter disappointment he felt when, instead of a copy of John D. Rockefeller's personal *New York Times*, Gilberto found that what they had sent him was a series of newspaper clippings.

Neither that day nor the following days was he able to find Paulo so he could read him the articles. The weekend was approaching, and with it an important game between Benfica and Porto. Gilberto would not have any free time until Sunday. Saturday's games were intense. Benfica defeated Porto 5-1 at the Amoreiras stadium, and took the lead in the tournament, one point ahead of Sporting, who had also won, beating Académica 3-0 at the Campo Grande stadium. Days like this, when there are two games in the city, complicate everything. If there's enough time, Gilberto goes to both. If not, he arranges to go to one game and find out the details about the other. That Saturday, not only did he go to both games and do the respective write-ups, but he also took down the highlights of the matches between Belenenses and Vitoria and Boavista and Carcavelinhos by phone at the newspaper office. The two pages on Sunday made Gilberto very proud, but they also gave him a chance to sleep in on Sunday, so much so that he barely had time to get ready to go to church with his family. That Sunday after lunch, Gilberto was finally able to think again about the package he had received and he went out looking for Paulo.

The poet was a man set in his ways, so it was easy for Gilberto to find him at the Luís Camões Plaza arguing with friends Gilberto did not know.

"Gilberto, come on, we are talking about Hauptmann's execution. Do you think he was really guilty?"

Based on how Paulo spoke to him, Gilberto concluded that the poet's interlocutors were not good friends of his. That's why he answered only that the law knows what it's doing. He sat down with the group and soon the meeting was over, which confirmed to him that this was not just a conversation to kill time on a Sunday. But Gilberto was not interested in getting involved in anything too deeply, these were complicated times to be going around asking too many questions.

When the last of the group left, Paulo persisted with the topic of the alleged murderer of the Lindbergh baby. "Do you really think the law knew what it was doing?" No, Gilberto had no idea what the law did on the other side of the ocean. He didn't even know much about the case other than the fact that the child was lost. Paulo then gave up and, at the feet of the statue of the great Camões, he looked through the articles that the Rockefeller Foundation had sent Gilberto.

"I'm afraid my English is not as good as I thought," said the poet, amused. The articles did have one thing in common with John D. Rockefeller's personal edition: they were articles from *The New York Times* about the old philanthropist.

Under the attentive watch of Luís de Camões, Paulo related to Gilberto that Rockefeller had gone on a car trip and had even posed for pictures during a 45-mile drive (however long that was), that his private secretary had married a girl by the name of Lee Sage Lockerde, from Hartford, Connecticut, that his only living daughter had gone to Ormond Beach for a ten-day visit, the same as the Miltons, and that the road trips had become a routine that the old man seemed to enjoy a lot.

Gilberto recounted these facts almost verbatim to Mr. Manso, who was surprised both by the fact that the story of Rockefeller's paper was still alive and by the disappointment he could hear in the young man's voice.

"Indeed, there is not a single indication here that the paper exists, but why would it?" asked Manso, and Gilberto did not know what to answer.

For about four months, he had been formulating theories about why Rockefeller had his own newspaper with custom-written news, and he had two favorites. The first was that the philanthropist was so obsessed with doing good, with giving away money to make the world a better place, that he didn't want to find out about the meager success of his efforts in a world plagued with economic problems and conflict. The second was that the fierce businessman of the past had made many enemies and, as an old man, did not want to risk coming across attacks on his person, not even in the pages of the newspaper. But neither of his theories fit with the image of the good-natured old man that he took from the news articles, the one who takes drives by the beach and is visited by family and friends.

The director of the newspaper didn't want his young writer to take this as a defeat. "Maybe the story needs a different approach," Manso said, "maybe what's interesting is why there are people so far away from the United States who think the multimillionaire tycoon has his own special editions written for him." Ever since Manso had heard the anecdote from Gilberto, it had seemed like nonsense invented by people who didn't have the slightest clue of how a newspaper worked, let alone one as big as *The New York Times*. Nonetheless, he wanted Gilberto to arrive at that conclusion by his own means, and, along the way, to perhaps find a story that was actually worth telling. Maybe the last days of old man Rockefeller, who was already 96, who would die at any moment, the man who built an oil empire, would have to be contrasted with the affable old guy who drives his car along the beaches of Daytona.

But Gilberto was not ready to build the story that he had received in the mail. And by now Manso was almost certain that he never would be. The story he was waiting for still loomed large in his mind.

Without any indications, without any clues, he couldn't do much to convince Mr. Manso that he could write the story. And even if he could write it, he wouldn't know what to write. Because, in the end, he was in complete agreement with the director of the *Diário*—there was no story, not yet. The question was whether there would be at some point, and whether it was worth waiting for.

However, the wait was short and ended unexpectedly. The next Sunday, Paulo went to Gilberto's house carrying the paper, not a copy of the *Diário de Lisboa*, but the *Diário de Notícias*, a morning paper rather than an evening edition like the one Gilberto worked for and one of the most widely distributed newspapers in Portugal. In it was an article stating that John D. Rockefeller received a copy of the fake *New York Times* containing "only pleasant news and optimistic articles."

Gilberto's first reaction was one of betrayal. He immediately suspected Mr. Manso and even Paulo himself, the only two people who knew about his plans to write about Rockefeller's paper. They must have mentioned it somewhere and, given their high profile, the conversation easily reached the ears of a reporter at the *Diário de Notícias*. But, after seeing Paulo's surprised face and re-reading the article, Gilberto's sentiment of betrayal gave way to a mixture of helplessness and frustration that took away the anger still nestled in his chest.

"They got the old guy's age wrong," was the only thing Gilberto managed to say, completely discouraged by the missed exclusive, unable to articulate anything other than the detail in the article stating that Rockefeller was 97 years old, when in reality the multimillionaire was still a few months away from his birthday.

The next day, back in Mr. Manso's office, Gilberto and his boss concluded that the *Diário de Notícias* hadn't had a lot to go on when writing the story.

"We could wait to see if you receive something else from the US," said Manso, in hopes that Gilberto wouldn't give up on the story, but without really expecting that the young man would continue to follow the elusive topic.

"What if I go to the *Diário de Notícias*?"

The question didn't sit well with the director of the *Diário de Lisboa*, who always jealously guarded his own news agenda and was incapable of jumping on board a topic simply because another paper had beaten him to it.

"Never trust an archived news story. If that's all they published, it's because that's all they had to publish. And if they did save something else to publish later, maybe because they couldn't run it at the time, they're not going to tell you about it."

Gilberto nodded. The disappointment on his face told Manso that the story was effectively dead. But Gilberto was resolved to go to the *Diário de Notícias* even if he had to hide it from his boss.

At the newspaper's headquarters, he asked for a colleague he knew from the stadium; but when he told him the reason for his visit, the colleague didn't take it well. He was left waiting for a long time, and when he was finally able to talk to the editor of the international section, the editor spoke only in the plural, shielded behind the anonymity of his sources, and only told him that they had received the news from South America.

We all have a cousin in South America, thought Gilberto as he considered the possibility of not repeating his epistolary investigation with newspapers from the Southern hemisphere and instead contacting acquaintances to ask for help. After all, they would have to start by finding out whether, in fact, some paper on that side of the ocean had published the story. Just thinking about the magnitude of the project, it seemed too much for him. It was clear now that the Rockefeller paper had become old and archived news.

Like all unwritten pages, the topic began to fade away with the help of reality and the daily bombardment of new stories. The Olympic Games in Berlin were approaching and Gilberto was ready to give them the best coverage possible.

If Rockefeller's paper had stayed alive, maybe Mr. Manso would have seen the same expression on Gilberto's face that he saw the day he told him to forget about going to the office of the *Diário de Notícias*. When Manso called him to a meeting on the topic, Gilberto never imagined it was simply to inform him that they had come to an agreement with the former soccer player and now sports reporter Antonio Ribeiro dos Reis, who would be in Berlin on his own, but who would send his contributions to the paper once a week. That was the only feature the *Diário de Lisboa* would run on the Olympic Games. Gilberto never expected to be sent to Berlin, he knew perfectly well that sports did not have an important place in the *Diário de Lisboa*, but the fact that there would not be any special plan besides one or two weekly chronicles seemed to him like a mistake, and he told the director so once Ribeiro dos Reis had left.

"There won't be any space for more, I'm sorry," was all Manso told him.

Gilberto's frustration increased during the event. The pages of the *Diário de Lisboa* were filled with stories about the Spanish Civil War and the tensions in the rest of Europe, and that was easy to understand, but more could have been done, and much better. Gilberto particularly disliked the coverage on fencing, a sport in which Portugal had high hopes. He followed it during the quarterfinals, and when Portugal made it to the semifinals he wrote the story. But a little later the same day, news broke of Portugal's elimination after losing to Sweden and Italy in the semifinals, and Gilberto wrote the story again. To his surprise, both pieces were published, one on page three, the other on page four. He had constantly been denied space, and now suddenly he had different pieces on different pages. The chronicles by Ribeiro dos Reis also enraged Gilberto, not because of the pieces themselves, which were fabulous, but because he did indeed send them once a week during an event that lasted two weeks and featured games every day. The chronicle on the opening ceremony was published four days after the fact. The track-and-field write-up was published after the competition had already concluded, and the last piece by Ribeiro appeared two days after Gilberto interviewed the Portuguese athletes once they had already returned home.

Gilberto knew that if he wanted to build a career as a sports reporter he had to leave the *Diário de Lisboa*. But life had better plans for him. He usually got together with Paulo at least once a week, and during one of those encounters he met the poet's younger sister, Constança. His attraction to her was instantaneous and that very afternoon Gilberto asked Paulo for permission to call on his sister.

"If I didn't think you were a good match, I'd never have let her meet you. But you still have to talk to her parents."

That's how he said it, "her parents," which took Gilberto by surprise, as though Constança and Paulo were siblings from different parents. Or maybe it was just poetic license on Paulo's part. In any case, the important thing is that Gilberto started visiting Constança twice a week. Gilberto visited the Salcido family every Wednesday for lunch. On Sundays, he would cut his family lunch short to go to the Salcidos' house again and then take a stroll with Constança, accompanied by a chaperone, of course, since Gilberto's intentions were honorable and there had to be evidence of it.

Because of the Sunday stroll, Gilberto's weekly outings with the poet, which had become indispensable ever since Paulo started reading and translating the articles he had received, were moved to Mondays instead.

One of those Mondays, Paulo translated the articles that arrived in the second package sent by the Rockefeller Foundation. Gilberto felt his old hope light up again, but it was soon extinguished. Rockefeller's trip to his residence in New Jersey, his trip back to Florida, a visit from a friend or relative, road trips, a few public appearances, his 97th birthday, the death of someone close to him, nothing worth publishing months afterward on the other side of the ocean.

The year 1937 arrived around this time, and when he received another envelope, Gilberto didn't even need a translation. It was almost the same news. After all, what else could be expected from an old man, regardless of how many millions he had at his disposal?

What would the director of the paper have said if he had seen the small newspaper library Gilberto had built to the rhythm of transatlantic mail? He had practically stopped talking to Mr. Manso after the Olympic Games. Manso never suspected that his silence was personal, immersed as he was in daily coverage of the events in Spain. Maybe if Gilberto had shown up one day in the director's office with his little stack of newspaper clippings, things would have taken a different course, but that never happened. It didn't happen because Gilberto didn't really know why he kept saving the newspaper clippings, but he knew for sure that he wouldn't do anything with them.

He didn't even open the last envelope. For Gilberto, Rockefeller had stopped being news, and if he had looked at the content of the correspondence, maybe he would have concluded that Rockefeller wasn't news for *The New York Times* either. The envelope contained only three news items: John D. Junior's March 16 visit to his father's residence at Ormond Beach, a road trip along the beach on the 28th of the same month that had to be interrupted because of unexpected high tides, though old man Rockefeller insisted on going back along the same beach rather than taking the highway, and the news on April 18th of instructions for the residence at Pocantico Hills, Rockefeller's summer house in White Plains, New York, to begin preparations to receive the multimillionaire on June 1.

But there was no longer a story, not for Gilberto, who months before had been just as convinced as Mr. Manso himself that they would never know whether the special edition of *The New York Times* actually existed. Quite honestly, Mr. Manso was certain from the beginning that it didn't, but Gilberto always kept up hope that it might, as long as he didn't receive a definitive confirmation otherwise. And who could offer that confirmation? Not just anyone, since the existence of something as personal as a custom-made newspaper can only be denied by someone in the know. Old man Rockefeller himself was, without a doubt, the best person to either confirm or deny the paper's existence, but between road trips to the beach and family visits he never found out that a newspaper editor from Lisbon had written the Foundation asking a rather strange question. Yes, it was certainly strange, especially in a world that demanded ever greater attention from all four directions.

The news that arrived from Spain, Germany, England, Ethiopia did not allow one to waste time finding out stupid details regarding the life of an old man, regardless of whether the old man was the first multimillionaire known in history. That's how Gilberto convinced himself that things had turned out for the best, and if the set of newspapers clippings was still there, messily filed in his bedroom, it was only there as a possible reminder that the story of Rockefeller's personal paper had never been worth it and that the only logical course of action was to let it fade into oblivion. There were better things to do. There will always be sports news, and even if Mr. Manso doesn't give them the importance Gilberto believes they deserve, they will still be published and Gilberto will still be there to write them.

Everything seemed perfect in Gilberto's life, but then that Monday arrived. On his way to the Bragança Hotel, the same kid as always handed him his copy of the *Diário de Lisboa* and, leafing through it immediately, he saw the picture and the caption.

Now, seated at the table after sending the telegram with his resignation, he read the picture's caption again and again he took it as a personal insult. Half a page, Gilberto could have written at least half a page, not as an homage to the dead old man, but to the work that he'd wanted to write and couldn't during the year and a half that had gone by since he first proposed to Mr. Manso, without desire and without conviction, it must be said, the story about the fake edition of *The New York Times* that John D. Rockefeller received. The desire and the conviction came afterward, but also the inability, and that was what offended Gilberto so deeply.

No, there is no turning back. The more he thinks and the more he goes over the events of the entire year, the more it offends him that they did not take the time to seek him out and ask him if he wanted to write about the death of the tycoon. An affront.

As soon as Paulo walked into the dinning room, Gilberto could see that he was carrying the *Diário de Lisboa*, just like the time he reprimanded him for the short news story about Fernando Pessoa's death. Paulo saw him, Gilberto showed him his own copy of the *Diário* while at the same time letting the poet know with his other hand and a slight discouraged nod that, in effect, it was all over. He noticed no disapproval in Paulo's reaction as he approached the table, although for a moment he supposed that, as his fiancée's brother, Paulo would have something to say about his rash decision and his now uncertain future. There will be time to think about Constança. For the moment, Paulo's company was enough. There was no better person with whom to share the feeling of being misunderstood than a poet whose work is unknown. 舌

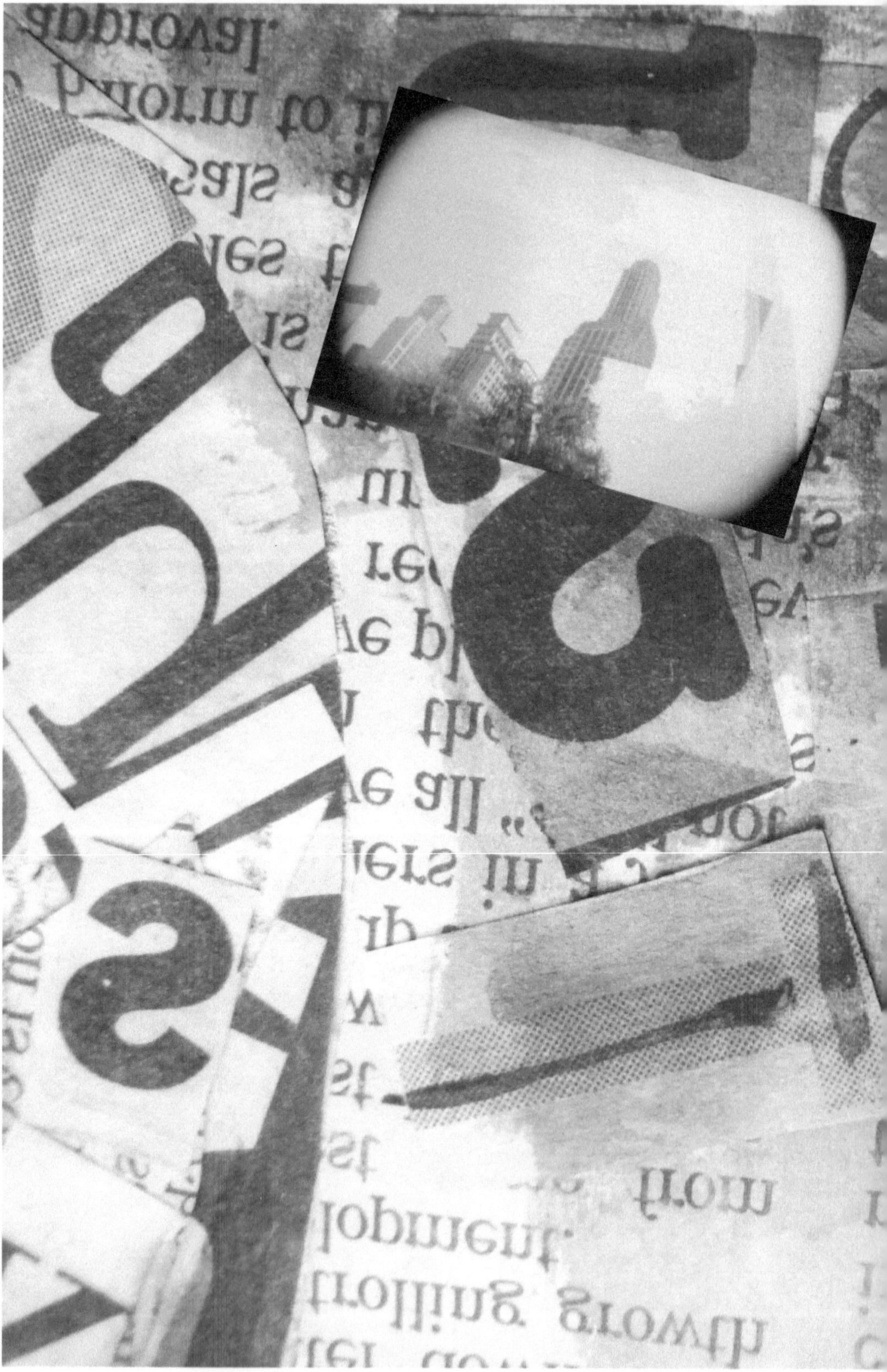

Caracas ~ Chicago

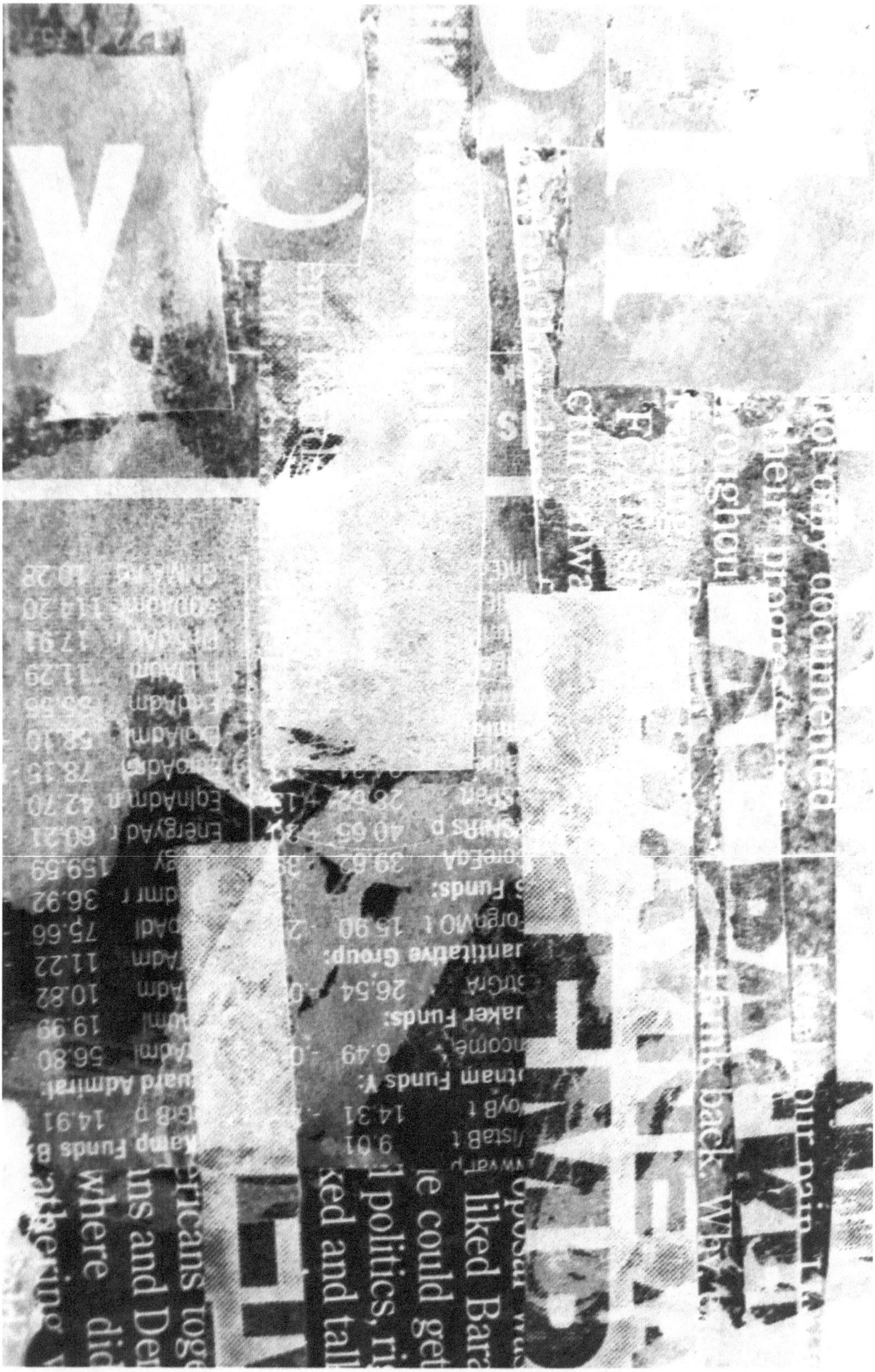

Few places in my house make me as anxious as the library. It is the place where all unfinished tasks accumulate, contained in the piles of books that are still unread. But above all, the library is the place where oblivion dwells. So many pages read that I don't remember, so many novels, short stories, poems that when I first read them seemed to change my life or fill it with profound happiness, with wonder, with mystery and even wisdom, all of which I am incapable of remembering now except, in the best of cases, in vague outlines, as though all those stories were destined to become reader's notes and nothing more. In the end, what I read, what I am, what I have read and what I will be are nothing but a string of phrases and moments that have managed to latch onto my memory and become part of me. In order to define who I am, in order to decipher myself, to reveal the true me, just a few sentences suffice. Not many.

Of the books that have stuck with me, few have done so for as long as *The Year of the Death of Ricardo Reis,* in which José Saramago makes Ricardo Reis, Fernando Pessoa's heteronym, reside among the living. In a unique game of mirrors, Pessoa's ghost appears before Reis, making the true person unreal and the character created by José Saramago real. Words become flesh, the poet as God's sibling, language that constructs a new reality and changes, substitutes, or cancels out true reality. There is no such thing as true reality because all reality depends on the words we use to construct it and every word is a symbol'it is matter that flows and cannot be grasped and sometimes cannot even be understood, at least not completely.

But, like so many other books, *The Year of the Death of Ricardo Reis* eventually began to transform itself into a series of isolated images that, set side by side, did not seem to relate to the book they came from. And from among all these images, there is one that has little to do with the novel itself, an anecdote unconnected to it although it is part of it.

The narrator tells us that Reis came across a story in the newspaper that surprised him. An avid consumer of the press, it is telling that this particular story was the one to incite the most thoughts and reflections in Reis. The story was about John D. Rockefeller, the old multimillionaire who received a special edition of *The New York Times* with only good news. Saramago writes that Reis dislikes not being able to choose the news he is given, unlike "a certain old American who every morning receives a copy of *The New York Times*, his favorite newspaper. It is a special edition, which guards the precarious health of the senile reader who has reached the ripe age of ninety-seven, because each day it is doctored from start to finish with nothing but good news and articles brimming with optimism, so that the poor old man will not be troubled by the world's disasters, which are likely to grow more disastrous..." Saramago writes that the old man is (was) "the sole inhabitant of a world privileged with a strictly individual and non-transferable happiness. The rest of mankind has to be satisfied with whatever remains." But what Reis experiences is admiration, astonishment, and, resting the Portuguese paper on his lap, he imagines John D. reading his paper with only good news, or fake news, because perhaps in 1936 one thing implied the other but they were completely different. Or maybe not.

Saramago turns all of us, or at least he turned me, into Ricardo Reis, at least a little, because it is difficult not to get caught up in the anecdote.

José Acosta is a Dominican writer who, on May 14, 2009—how precise is the internet?—published a short story on his blog entitled "Rockefeller's Newspaper." The story is directly inspired by the anecdote in Saramago's novel, and the anecdote also serves as an epigraph to Acosta's story, in which Rockefeller finds out about the lies in *The New York Times* through the details of daily life, like a mistaken weather report and the robbery of a jewelry store that the old multimillionaire witnesses from his apartment in Richford thanks to his binoculars.

In Acosta's story, Rockefeller receives an anonymous note trying to warn him about the lies in *The New York Times*, which would imply that the existence of the fake edition is *vox populi*, except, of course, for the old philanthropist who, just as Saramago notes in *The Year of the Death of Ricardo Reis*, is "...unaware that they are telling him lies. Everyone else knows it, because the deception has been telegraphed by news agencies from continent to continent, that in the editorial offices of *The New York Times* orders have been issued to suppress all bad news..." *The New York Times* reports the existence of a fake *New York Times*, another game of mirrors in the novel, just like Pessoa's ghost conversing with the real Reis. But Saramago is not interested in the effect the fake *New York Times* has on the real *New York Times*. What interests him is the effect the helpless multimillionaire has on other mortals: "Such a wealthy and powerful man allowing himself to be fooled in this way, and fooled twice, because not only do we know that what he thinks he knows is false, but we also know that he'll never know what we know."

The year when Reis reads the news about Rockefeller is 1936. Rockefeller will die the following year and in 1941 a movie will come out about a super powerful, solitary, repentant man on his deathbed, *Citizen Kane*, and even if Orson Welles's film is based not on Rockefeller but on publishing tycoons of the era, the idea of a multimillionaire who remembers the most minimal details of his childhood or who is incapable of witnessing the horrors of the world, horrors that he perhaps helped to create, was presumably a popular topic during Welles's times.

In his 2013 novel *The Reputations,* Colombian author Juan Gabriel Vásquez echoes the anecdote as unconfirmed news, as a memory not contested on Google: "Wasn't it Rockefeller who had his own version of *The New York Times,* an adulterated version from which all bad news had been eliminated?" One thing is completely different in the way Vásquez refers to the affair. It would have been Rockefeller himself who decided to receive a newspaper with only good news. In fact, Vásquez elaborates on this, and the main character in his novel, Javier Mallarino, believes that the rage, indignation, and hatred he feels when reading undesirable news is the energy that keeps him alive and he cannot give it up. It is not for nothing that Mallarino is a renowned cartoonist, which establishes a sort of link between his profession and Rockefeller's paper. He transforms the news that would have been unlikely—very unlikely—to have appeared in Rockefeller's *New York Times* into an object of scorn and laughter. Reis is bothered by the fact that he cannot choose the news he receives, which is why he envies Rockefeller in a way. The news Mallarino receives in the headquarters of the newspaper bothers him too, and he doesn't understand how Rockefeller opted out of such unpleasantries.

But in Vásquez, Acosta, and Saramago, the emphasis falls on the reader of the good-newspaper. What effect did it have on Rockefeller, on his vision of the world during his last years, either knowingly or naïvely reading only the good news contained in his own edition of *The New York Times*? What effect would it have on us? And, above all, how does the helpless Rockefeller, unaware of the truth of the world, fare before us, reliable witnesses to reality?

Just as in *Citizen Kane,* in the good-newspaper there is commiseration for the millionaire. It makes us feel pity that, in spite of his power, he cannot tolerate the news of the world as it actually is. Rockefeller will die having amassed one of the greatest fortunes in history, but he was unable to look at the first page of the newspaper without it first being altered, the poor man.

I was always interested in the anecdote from a different perspective, the perspective of the false edition's editors.

The news of the fake edition of *The New York Times* does not seem to have reached *The New York Times*, contrary to what Saramago thought. In the archive of the newspaper there is nothing regarding either false or fake editions of the paper. There are no references to the matter among the sadly notorious cases of the newspaper's bad practices either, and I think we could include a paper containing only fake news among the instances of bad journalism, regardless of whether it had been ordered by the readers themselves, or even because of this.

There isn't much news from the Rockefellers regarding the matter either. In 2008, I had a brief email exchange with Ken Rose regarding some research I did on the Rockefeller Archive Center. One of my questions was regarding the veracity of the anecdote and, if it was true, whether any copies of the good-newspaper existed.

As Assistant Director of the Archive Center, Rose answered me, cc'ing Judy Russo, saying the idea that Rockefeller received a special edition of *The New York Times* was most likely a product of José Saramago's imagination, and that in the over twenty years that he'd been working at the Rockefeller Family Archive, he'd never come across either the story or a copy of the special edition. Rose ended his message by asking me, out of personal curiosity, what Saramago novel I was talking about. I answered him, offering to provide more information if I came across any new details on the matter.

My next task was writing the Fundação José Saramago about the source from which the author had obtained his anecdote. In a more institutional than personal manner, unlike the email from Rose, Rita Pais answered that Saramago had obtained his references from the Portuguese newspapers of his era and that, therefore, the story of Rockefeller's paper was not a product of the author's imagination but of a news story from the time.

Hence, the project consisted not only of finding a copy of *The New York Times* especially written for and sent to John D. Rockefeller, or even just a more official reference to it, but also of finding the news story that Saramago read and would have Ricardo Reis read.

In the novel, Saramago usually refers to the press in plural or in generic terms. Reis reads the newspapers, the paper, the morning or the evening press, occasionally a specific paper in which Reis finds a news item referenced. A few newspapers are mentioned, like the satirical daily *Os Ridículos*, the *Diário de Notícias* and *O Século*, but the facts that Reis finds are mentioned in lists without being attributed to any particular paper—after all, the plot is about someone reading the press of the day, with the added difficulty of Saramago's characteristic punctuation, which goes on subordinate clause after clause to the point that one sometimes loses track of the facts to which he's referring.

Ricardo Reis took advantage of the sunny morning to sit and read the paper at Alto de Santa Catarina, at the feet of the great Adamastor, the monument celebrating Luís de Camões. That day Reis found out about the existence of a newspaper especially written for John D. Rockefeller, and the Brazilian doctor also read about the Italian-Ethiopian war, the mass strike in Madrid, the official time change, a new apparition of the Loch Ness Monster, the debut of a newspaper entitled *O Crime*, and the death of Ottorino Respighi, among other news. This last fact makes the research easy: it must be the morning of April 19, 1936, taking into account that the Italian composer died on the 18th. On April 19, 1936, Ricardo Reis, Fernando Pessoa's heteronym, read that John

D. Rockefeller received an adulterated version of *The New York Times*.

This is as far as I got for the moment, constrained by the impossibility of reviewing the Rockefeller family's personal archives or Portuguese press libraries.

Research is not a random voyage, even if during the voyage unexpected twists might occur. Who knows how long ago popular knowledge declared that there are no fruitless searches with the maxim "seek and ye shall find," as if the end result of every investigation were determined by its origins and not by whatever might be obtained during its development. I ended my research because of what I thought was a lack of resources. Over time, I realized that I lacked clear goals. I didn't know what story I wanted to tell. Rockefeller's anecdote was an excuse, an excuse for something else, to discover its origin, recreate its development, speculate about its outcome, all of the above. The heart of the matter was in Mr. Rose's email. He had cut my initial drive short. I wanted to see those copies of *The New York Times*. I wanted to see the news it contained, what type of information it offered each morning to the old man.

Saramago imagined completely fictitious news, the easing of the financial crisis, the end of unemployment, the evolution of Bolshevik Russia toward a more American system, a harmonious world. But a newspaper like that demanded much more elaboration than the one imagined by Vásquez, an edition that was merely mutated, with gaps regarding the advance of communism, fascist upheavals, the aftermath of the Crash of 1929 that reduced Rockefeller's own capital so much. It is not the paper Acosta imagined either, one with more local news like a weather forecast that Rockefeller would enjoy, or the absence of events like the robbery of local jewelry store. Considered fairly, Acosta's *New York Times* is a paper like any other, one that gets the weather forecast wrong and refrains from writing about certain news items because of its rather limited interest. Vásquez's *New York Times* is an abridged one, not very different from the morning report that the director of any industry or the manager of an institution with specific interests would receive, as though Rockefeller's personalized version of *The New York Times* was nothing more than a daily summary of newspaper articles on the achievements and activities of the Rockefeller Foundation, which by the year of the philanthropist's death had contributed some $530 million from the Gold Standard to a wide variety of causes. Saramago's *New York Times* was a work of fiction, of science fiction, anticipating the future and reconstructing it through language so that it could end up resembling what the only reader of the utopian publication wanted. But what did the true edition of the fake *New York Times* look like?

All things considered, had one of those copies arrived in my hands, the whole affair would have ended. After all, it would be a historical document, a copy of what is perhaps the most famous newspaper in the world caricatured by the publishers themselves. With a copy of Rockefeller's *New York Times* before me, at most I could have looked over its news items and categorized them into completely invented stories and stories that had only been adulterated. I could have compared, perhaps, the transformation of the Soviet system that Saramago's *New York Times* talks about with the real fall of the Soviet block. *The New York Times* imagined by Saramago itself offered interesting predictions, since *The Year of the Death...* came out before 1989. But, going back to my original idea, having those copies in my possession would have been the start of a grand project, a combination of a research project and a novel, something in between fiction, meta-fiction, and reality. I would have looked for the edition's creators in the newspaper's stain; I would have reconstructed their lives before and especially after the apocryphal *New York Times*; I would have recreated the creative process required to come up with every issue, every story, every lie, and, in the end, I would have looked for the effects that reading the fake newspaper had on old man Rockefeller, the tycoon's true reaction, not the one imagined by Saramago, Acosta, and Vásquez.

That's why Rose's response was so disappointing. If issues of the false or adulterated *New York Times* didn't exist, then my interest in narrating what they might have contained or what might have happened to them didn't exist either. That's what I thought, but I was totally mistaken.

The question stayed on my mind, along with the other, although the second question gained more and more traction as time went by: What was the origin of the story Ricardo Reis read? Answering one question didn't imply answering the other, researching one was an independent task from researching the other, and they both had led me to what appeared to be a dead end.

However, like water that builds a solid stalagmite drop by drop, stalled time began to mold the characters who would tell the story, the story of the writer of the special *New York Times* and the story of the reporter who would report the news in a Portuguese newspaper. Suddenly, the investigation was not about facts, editions that had been published or not, but about settings, in New York and Lisbon in the 1930s. This story was completely different from the one that had motivated me up to that point. I found a novel, albeit a different one from the one I had started out searching for. To my surprise, I could not begin writing it because I had not been able to resolve, or at least satisfactorily conclude, my initial investigation. A few years after our first email exchange, I tried to contact Mr. Rose, only to discover that he had died. I had simply wanted to share with him the decisive role he had played in the direction my project took, and also to ask him if the curiosity he had shown for the book in which Saramago had written the anecdote had actually motivated him to get a copy of *The Year of the Death of Ricardo Reis* and read it. I had a vague hope that Rose would be interested in the same thing that spurred me on at the time: the origin of the story. If Rose was right, the story published in the Portuguese paper was an invention or a rumor from the era.

I have always been attracted to this kind of story. On May 9, 2002, the defunct Spanish online magazine en.red.ando published my article "Where is Orson Welles?" in which I relate several stories of false attribution that were going around the internet at the time and in which I quote a sentence from a movie titled *Midnight in the Garden of Good and Evil* that says, "Truth, like art, is in the eye of the beholder."

This is more or less the same as the premise I use in my short story "Operation We Love Borges So Much," in which an author tries to perpetuate the false attribution of the poem "Instants" to Jorge Luis Borges, because there is no doubt that "Instants" is a great poem if signed by Borges, but a mediocre poem if signed by its true author.

I am always surrounded by rumor. In a story titled "The Unexpected Death of Mickey Mouse," the narrator refers to the famous freezing of Walt Disney, while in "Chavela," one character asks another whether saying a rumor has been confirmed means the information passed along by the rumor is true or the rumor is indeed going around.

Rumor is evasive by nature. It is evasive because every good rumor is made of stories we wish were true, whether because they're beautiful or because they're abject. The veracity of what the rumor tells us is, above all, the desire of the person who listens and repeats. If the desire is strong, then there is no denying it. Rumor is transmitted as an act of faith.

This is why I could not easily give up discovering the truth behind Rockefeller's *New York Times*. The fiction I created was not enough; it was incomplete without the story of the search.

When I restarted the project, several things had recently occurred. The most important was the fact that the digitization of archives had achieved impressive magnitudes. The second, no less decisive, was that Venezuela had become a country of emigrants, and even if my first messages to the Rockefeller Archive Center and the Fundação José Saramago were sent from Caracas, the message to my friend Maida originated in Chicago and was received in Madeira.

In a Facebook message, I asked Maida if she could look in the National Library of Portugal for any newspapers from April 19, 1936, and she replied with links to the online editions of the Portuguese press, which she quickly found because her mother-in-law works at the regional archive in Madeira.

Thus, I had before me the April 19, 1936 issue of the *Diário de Lisboa*. I was soon able to see that the paper had published nothing that day regarding the interesting fact that the American multimillionaire John D. Rockefeller received a special edition of *The New York Times* with nothing but good news.

But I had a lot of information to go over, and in the Lisbon Municipal Digital Library I found the first issue of *O Crime* magazine, which Ricardo Reis knew had been published that very day, Sunday, April 19, 1936.

O Crime didn't live very long. It only published six issues, or at least that's how many the Lisbon Municipal Library has. The problem, from the point of view relevant to me, is that the date of the first issue is April 18, 1936. The novel is clear—Ricardo Reis was sitting down reading the newspaper at Alto de Santa Catarina, and he read, among other things, that that day the first issue of *O Crime* had hit the stands and that Ottorino Respighi had died. Indeed, the magazine came out the same day as the death of Respighi, but the news of his death couldn't have appeared in papers the same day, unless it was an evening paper, and even then it would have been difficult for the news to make the evening edition.

I went over the April 18th issue of the *Diário de Lisboa* and I found another story Reis had read that day, the one about the time change. I also found that the mass strike in Spain had ended. Looking at the April 17th issue, I found the start of the mass strike and the publication of *O Crime* the following day.

I then had the feeling that Ricardo Reis had read the papers from several days on that same morning. There was nothing strange about this—in fact, in several instances throughout the novel, Reis gets up to date by reading several papers at once. But that is not the case in this particular passage. Reis rests the paper, one paper, on his lap to think about Rockefeller's *New York Times*, and the scene ends with the Brazilian doctor leaving the paper, not the papers, for the two old men he used to see at the park who always waited for Reis to leave the finished paper on the bench so they could hurry over and claim it for themselves.

For the first time, I faced the possibility that José Saramago might not have had Reis read a specific paper, but rather a weekend summary, like some sort of world almanac. After all, Saramago was reflecting the spirit of the era in which Reis read. That would also explain why the references in most cases are to newspapers, to the press in general, and not to a newspaper in particular, since readers usually have their favorite paper and, even if they read several papers, they tend to always either start with one or save one for last. They also know which they will read and which they won't if they're short on time, and they even know which they'll favor if they find contradicting versions of the same information. Which paper did Ricardo Reis read first? Which one did he read last? Which did he favor if he didn't have time to read them all? Which one did he think had more authority?

These are questions that are not in the novel, which is why they are left unanswered, because Ricardo Reis is a character of Pessoa's and Saramago's imagination.

If Saramago based Reis's newspaper readings on a compilation of important news and events and not on specific issues, then I wouldn't necessarily be successful reading every newspaper published in Portugal the weekend of April 17-19, 1936. Even now, reading all the Portuguese news from that weekend is still an unfinished task. I have not been able to access the two most important papers in the country at that time, the *Diário de Notícias* and *O Século*. I have the addresses and archive schedules of both, in anticipation of a trip to Portugal that would allow me to view them, since neither has online access. Maybe in one of those two newspapers is the telegram Saramago read, and which he had Ricardo Reis read in his novel. Maybe not, in which case the mystery of the special edition of *The New York Times* that was custom-written and edited especially for John D. Rockefeller will become even more complicated. Maybe everything I have written has no meaning as I have not yet found the telegram. Maybe reading it is not so necessary in the end.

As though leading us to information weren't enough, now Google aims to possess all of it and to somehow become its owner. A couple of years ago, it would have been impossible to find the information I now had in front of me, directly from Google Books.

Julio Eugui seems more like a priest than a writer. He has written several books on Christian wisdom and the love of God and our fellow humans, but I was unable to find even the smallest biographical detail about Eugui himself, no news stories about the presentation or baptism of a new book, not even a picture from a book jacket. But fragments of his books were on Google Books, and they come up if one enters the right words in the search engine. In a book published in 2004, *One Thousand Anecdotes of Virtue*, Eugui mentions Rockefeller's good tidings newspaper, but its source is not *The Year of the Death of Ricardo Reis* but rather a press article by Juan Carlos Onetti entitled what else but "Good News."

Onetti's article is from 1985 and was published in the Spanish newspaper *ABC*, where Onetti was a columnist. In it, he mentions the good news, which was the result of a contract between the

Rockefeller family and *The New York Times* and from which old John D. would read only "the front page dedicated to news from abroad." Onetti says that *The New York Times* Rockefeller received "was always a sweet Christmas song, an unchangeable story of peace and eternal joy," but he gives the paper a different motivation, because in it there is "Nothing that could be disturbing, no rebellion in the slave countries who, due to a Divine Baptist or Methodist error, owned the oil that, reasonably, should only lie beneath Texas soil or in any other place in the great Northern democracy. This to save on freight, payoffs to dark-skinned members of the military, contraband, and coup d'états."

In Onetti's paper, as well as in Saramago's, it is the Rockefeller family who tries to keep the old man from the displeasure the outside world could cause him. But in Saramago's version, there is a fear of the current state of affairs. The advance of communism was a fear that many Americans of the era could share with the multimillionaire John D., even when the majority had to make do with not reading the papers instead of receiving a personal edition. However, the fear in Onetti's version has to do with the business practices of Standard Oil, especially during its beginning stages, which makes the Uruguayan author imagine an old John D. as a sort of Ebenezer Scrooge with a press at his disposal to chase away, every morning, the ghosts that appeared to him in the night.

In fact, Onetti's paper talks about a whole conspiracy to show us Rockefeller as a helpless old man with a benign biography. Yes, it is difficult to reconcile the philanthropist of the second half of his life with the shark of the first. There are several theories that speak of guilt as the primary motivation for Rockefeller's charitable spirit, although in his defense, that feature is also attributed to other captains of American industry, pioneers who alongside John D. created important initiatives of social retribution. There are those who deny this, as Rockefeller showed charitable impulses and intents even before becoming a successful, implacable oilman; his behavior as a philanthropist and as a predator even manifested itself several times in what we could call a simultaneous way. What does seem to be true is that, once he left control of Standard Oil in the hands of John D. Jr., the old man led a very charitable life, dedicating himself to philanthropic causes, his church, and golf, which he kept playing until he was over 90 years old.

Rockefeller died peacefully in his home at Ormond Beach, on the Atlantic coast of northern Florida. He died in a rather surprising way—as surprising as death can be for a 97-year-old—as none of his close family members were at Ormond Beach at the moment and the old man was preparing for a trip to New Jersey to celebrate his 98th birthday.

Looking through the 1936 and 1937 editions of *The New York Times*, which could have been the source of news of "another" *New York Times*, one can read stories about a John D. Rockefeller who had health problems natural to his age and who lived a life that was somewhat hidden from public view, but who was also active, taking road trips and traveling to his mansions in Richmond and Ormond Beach. I have not found anything that could lead me to confidently imagine a Rockefeller who tried to keep the world from entering to disturb him, nor that the efforts of his family to keep the old man from displeasure or annoyance were very different from the care any other family would take regarding their aging grandfather or grandmother.

But Onetti's article contains other items of interest. The first is simply the style. Reading it, it feels choppy, as though it were the victim of bad editing. The reference to the good-newspaper interrupts the narrative. It feels forced, and its purpose is difficult to understand. If I read the article skipping the two paragraphs in which the special *New York Times* is mentioned, the article is clearer, even though Onetti ends by asking us to help him create a good-newspaper for him. To a certain extent, Onetti allies himself with John D. After reading the current events of 1985. Who wouldn't want to receive only good news like old man Rockefeller?

Nonetheless, the article has two topics in one, the good-newspaper and the alleged attempt to write a good biography of John D. Rockefeller, the conspiracy I mentioned some paragraphs before. The author of an unauthorized biography would have been a publicist for Standard Oil, a man named John Doe, who achieved financial stability by writing an initial biography in which Rockefeller's past as an unscrupulous and exploitative businessman was omitted, but who afterwards, as a result of remorse and the end of the economic bonanza, wrote a second biography in which he told the whole truth. This biography would have been picked up from bookstores by "anonymous and generous men," leaving Rockefeller as "the doer of good deeds, the founder and baptizer of his celebrated Foundation. Another philanthropist of the prolific USA," for the rest of history. It is difficult, at least for me, to understand Onetti's point of view, first because in the end he seems to sympathize with Rockefeller and his good-newspaper, second because the philanthropist never completely prevailed over the predator in the public's eye. It is simply not true, and I think Onetti knew that he was simply telling a false story, a rumor or a myth, as it is not for nothing that he attributes both biographies to John Doe, the name given in the US to generic and unknown identities, or those that have to be protected. To talk about John Doe as the author of the biographies is a way of saying that anyone could have written those biographies; that is, they were common thoughts people had when referring to Rockefeller, the good guy, and Rockefeller, the bad. But the reference to John Doe allowed me to find another John: John K. Winkler.

Another mysterious character. Not even a Wikipedia entry exists on Winkler and the only personal information I could find was the death notice published in August 1958 in, where else, *The New York Times*, in which we learn that the author and biographer died at 67 years of age and that he had gained a certain fame between 1928 and 1955 for his works, including his 1929 book, *John D.: A Portrait in Oils*.

Rockefeller's biography appears even in the catalog of the Rockefeller Foundation library, but apparently the only thing left of the author is his death notice. In the oil portrait—oil was a better choice, to preserve the word game of the original title—Rockefeller looks truly bad. It is authentic libel, and thus it would not be surprising that the author had been subjected to oblivion by an operation like the one Onetti insinuates.

In any case, Winkler's vengeance did not lie in the fact that his small biography can still be found and read, or that ideas from it can be recognized in fragments of biographical sketches of the old John D. after his death, but in the effect that it seems to have had on the minds of readers.

Winkler tells us that Rockefeller reads *The New York Times* or has it read to him in the mornings, and *The New York Evening Post* in the evenings, but that the newspapers really tell him very little. If he wanted, the old John D. could publish the most interesting newspaper in the world by referencing the great number of reports he receives from all parts of the world. Rockefeller, Winkler adds, reads only the highlights because he likes to receive an advance summary of anything important that is happening in the world.

As I said, the book was published in 1929, a little before or almost simultaneously with the collapse of the New York Stock Exchange and the ensuing Great Depression. I don't know if that reference and the great events of the era gave way to a version of Rockefeller reading reports and summaries without the bad news of the time, but it seems possible. It is also possible that, as he grew to be a more helpless old man, the version was transformed to one in which he received his favorite newspaper without any of the news that most disturbed him.

Is Winkler's biography the true origin of John D. Rockefeller's personal edition of *The New York Times*? I don't know with certainty, and even if I did, the task of finding out how the rumor reached Europe and stayed alive to be mentioned during the 80s, almost 60 years after Winkler's book was published, will remain a pending task. What I do know is that the search would lead to South America.

With the project almost ready, I find myself talking with my friend and editor Fernando Olszanski, an Argentinian, who, after I mention to him what *The Last New York Times* is about, tells me that the same thing happened with an Argentinian president. I go back to Google and the first article I find about Hipólito Yrigoyen's newspaper is a categorical denial. Ángel J. Harman writes that the good-newspaper was part of a smear campaign that Yrigoyen's enemies undertook in order to justify the coup d'état they were planning, alleging that the president was senile and being manipulated. We are talking about Yrigoyen's second term in office, which began in 1929 and ended with the coup d'état in 1930.

This coincidence regarding the dates makes one think this is the same rumor, which went around targeting the most convenient powerful old man within reach. The "Good News Daily" is a topic in itself, but I only learned about it when I was already committed to Rockefeller's.

There is a third important detail in Onetti's article, and the most relevant one to my project. The article was published on Saturday, May 26, 1985. *The Year of the Death of Ricardo Reis* was published in Portugal in 1984 and arrived in Spain in 1985. Immediately the question rises about whether Onetti had read Rockefeller's anecdote in Saramago's novel and, if so, whether he read it before or after writing his article. Based on the difference in tone of the two versions, my feeling is that the references were conceived in parallel to each other and not one as a result of the other.

All things considered, a millionaire who cannot witness the world as it is, defeated by reality and incapable of changing it except on the first page of his paper, is a story that goes well with the mood of the 80s. Reagan and Thatcher dominate the world scene to the point of becoming a doctrine in and of themselves, while the Soviet Union shows signs of tiredness and decay that will lead to its dissolution before the end of the decade. It is a world in crisis and, in case that wasn't enough, a world under threat of disappearing at any moment due to a nuclear hecatomb. Anybody would have wanted, as Onetti observes, not to have to read so much upsetting news, not to have to feel so much disquietude when sipping the first cup of coffee in the morning or taking a break in the afternoon to be able to face the rest of the day. Even Rockefeller preferred that.

As I write this, the definitive news of the death of the Loch Ness Monster has circulated around the world. Nobody is claiming to have seen it anymore. In the era of Instagram, there are no pictures showing the monster allegedly photographed, and over 90 years have passed since its last official sighting. But does the death of the monster imply the death of the myth?

A new sighting of the Loch Ness Monster was one of the news items Reis read that morning of April 18, 1936, the same day the Brazilian doctor found out about the existence of the special *New York Times* read by John D. Rockefeller. Two myths live side by side in the pages of a newspaper read by a character of double creation by a poet and a novelist. Apparently, the Loch Ness Monster is dying or is dead, not of old age, but of diminution. Meanwhile, every now and then, Rockefeller's *New York Times* is re-edited by a writer's imagination. Saramago, Onetti, Vásquez, Acosta, and Eugui make up a sort of a secret literary club: the editors of

Rockefeller's *New York Times*. Mine is the last edition until another writer arrives and, trapped by the magic of the anecdote, imagines John D. Rockefeller reading a newspaper containing only fake news written especially for him. ▨

Acknowledgements

With projects that take so many years to finish, sometimes it is difficult to know where to start saying thank you. But, for this book it is easy, and that place is the third part of the novel and all the people I mention in it.

First, Fernando Olszanski, he not only has been fundamental for my literary career here in the United States, but he gave me the key detail to build the end of the novel. Second, the late Ken Rose, whose email reply was the beginning of what became The Last New York Times; this book always will have one less reader than it should have. Rita Pals' emails also were very important for the building process of this idea, and my good friend Maida Gomes gave me access to the archives I needed to search to understand what I was trying to write.

Julio Rangel gave the book a deep and insightful reading; all his recommendations were incorporated in the final version of this story.

Hernán Vera Álvarez read the book and became a strong force behind its original Spanish publication along with Pedro Medina León and Gaston Virkel from Suburbano as they continue working to bring new readers to it in our mother tongue.

This English version exists only by virtue of the enthusiasm and generosity of José Ángel Navejas, who put all his talent into translating the novel without any promise of seeing the result in the form of a book. Katelyn O'Brien performed excellent work reading the English version, knowing I could not read it with the eye for detail needed, along with Arthur M. Dixon who provided additional review and correction. Omar Villasana has been a patient and passionate editor, who took the risk to bring this book to a totally new audience.

Last but not least, thank you to my wife and daughter for being a fundamental part of everything I do. 五

About the author

Luis Alejandro Ordóñez (1973) is a Venezuelan writer who lives in the United States since 2008. Between Chicago and Miami he has worked as editor, copywriter, proofreader, translator, Spanish teacher and bookseller. In 2018 he published the Spanish version of *The Last New York Times* (Suburbano ediciones) and in 2015 a short stories collection titled *Play* (Editorial Ars Communis). He has been part of anthologies of writers who live in the United States and write in Spanish, such as *Diáspora* (Editorial Vaso Roto), *Pertenencia* and *Trasfondos* (both of Ars Communis) and *Escritorxs Salvajes* (Hypermedia Editores). In 2014 he won the II literary prize in Spanish from NorthEastern Illinois University for the story *Doble Negación*. With *Librero*, he won the Severo Ochoa Micro-Story Contest of the library of the Cervantes Institute in Chicago. He has collaborated with different websites, magazines and newspapers such as Suburbano, South Side Weekly, Univision, contratiempo, El Beisman, MiamiDiario, El Nacional, Producto magazine, among others. Web site: www.laoficinadeluis.com. ⌗

About the translator

José Ángel Navejas is the author of *Illegal: Reflections of an undocumented Immigrant* (2014) and *Invierno* (2019). He has edited *Palabras migrantes: 10 ensayistas mexican@s de Chicago* (2018). His forthcoming title, *Un mojado en Chicago y tres discursos inaugurales*, will be published by katakana editores. Currently, he is a PhD candidate at the University of Illinois at Chicago. ⊞

katakana
editores

Sello editorial sin fines de lucro.
Ediciones bilingües para enlazar culturas.

Non for profit publishing company.
Bilingual editions to bridge cultures

HISTORIA

Nuestra editorial katakana editores nace el 23 de abril de 2017 con
la publicación de la antología bilingüe de autores mexicanos Tiempos Irredentos/Unrepentant Times con prólogo de la Premio Cervantes 2013 Elena Poniatowska Amor y se funda formalmente el
día 31 de enero de 2018. 力

MISIÓN

Katakana editores tiene como misión conectar a lectores con es-
critores alrededor del mundo a través de (pero no limitado) las tra-
ducciones de sus obras al inglés, así como del inglés a otros idio-
mas como el español. 力

KATAKANA EDITORES CATALOGUE
CATALOGO KATAKANA EDITORES

KATAKANA EDITORES CATALOGUE
CATALOGO KATAKANA EDITORES
KATAKANA EDITORES CATALOGUE
CATALOGO KATAKANA EDITORES
KATAKANA EDITORES CATALOGUE
CATALOGO KATAKANA EDITORES
KATAKANA EDITORES CATALOGUE
CATALOGO KATAKANA EDITORES
KATAKANA EDITORES CATALOGUE
CATALOGO KATAKANA EDITORES
KATAKANA EDITORES CATALOGUE
CATALOGO KATAKANA EDITORES
KATAKANA EDITORES CATALOGUE
CATALOGO KATAKANA EDITORES
KATAKANA EDITORES CATALOGUE

POETRY CROSSOVER
(Bilingual poetry)

Among the Ruins/Entre las ruinas

(English/Spanish)
George Franklin (author).
Ximena Gómez (translator).
2018. 108 pages.
(Available in Kindle Format)
$12.00 usd ISBN-13: 978-1732114449

George Franklin's poems come from a deep understanding of human condition and beauty. Just like Tolstoi's short story where Jesus finds that even a dead dog can have teeth as white as pearls, George enlightens us with images of crows, moles, flies or spiders. There is also a soothing element in his writing even in moments of despair that bind an ancient Chinese poet to a woman whose child cannot accept the terrible effects of old age. Among the Ruins/Entre las ruinas depicts a world that sometimes seems in the verge of collapse but that redeems itself under the readers' eyes, when we allow poetry speak for itself. 田

Los poemas de George Franklin provienen de un profundo conocimiento de la naturaleza humana y la belleza. Tal como los relatos de Tolstoi cuando Jesús es capaz de encontrar en un perro muerto dientes tan blancos como las perlas, George nos ilumina con imágenes de cuervos, topos, moscas o arañas. También existe un elemento reconfortante en su escritura, aún en momentos desesperanzadores, capaces de unir a un antiguo poeta chino con una mujer cuyo hijo no puede aceptar los efectos de la vejez. Among the Ruins/ Entre las ruinas, nos muestra un mundo que por momentos parece encontrarse al borde del colapso pero que se redime bajo los ojos del lector cuando permitimos que la poesía hable por si misma. 𝍕

Último día/Last Day

(Spanish/English)
Ximena Gomez (autor)
George Franklin (translator)
2019. 114 pages
$12.00 usd
ISBN-13: 978-1732114470

Al mundo de Último día de Ximena Gómez se llega por veredas que la autora traza con precisión y delicadeza magistrales, con un pincel a la vez exquisito y escatológico. Este es un libro escuchado en susurros, un inventario minucioso del espacio que alberga el duelo, la ausencia, y hasta el amor: pequeños ruidos, sombras que esbozan en callado forcejeo las figuras de los que están, y de los que se han ido.

Francisco Larios (poeta y traductor, Compilador de la antología de poetas norteamericanos del Siglo XXI Los hijos de Whitman). 𝍕

We reach the world of Ximena Gómez's Last Day through paths that the author traces with masterful precision and delicacy, with a brushstroke that is both exquisite and eschatological. This is a book heard in whispers, a meticulous inventory of the space that houses mourning, absence, and even love: small noises, shadows that sketch in quiet struggle the figures of those who are present, and those who have gone.

Francisco Larios (poet and translator, compiler of the anthology of American poets of the XXI century Los hijos de Whitman) 舌

FICTION CROSSOVER
(bilingual fiction)

Tiempos Irredentos/Unrepentant Times

(Spanish/English)
Short stories by Mexican authors
Omar Villasana (editor)
George Henson, Arthur M. Dixon, José Armando Garcia, Silvia Guzmán (translators).
2017. 124 pages.
$16.95 usd.
ISBN-13: 978-0692884133

Seis relatos violentos de autores mexicanos: Alberto Chimal, Erika Mergruen, Yuri Herrera, Isaí Moreno, Úrsula Fuentesberain, Lorea Canales.

"En cada una de las historias prevalece la originalidad y el gozo de la escritura, rasgos que distinguen a los autores, pero también está presente la violencia, móvil de cada uno de los relatos y que fue la consigna bajo la cual mi amigo Omar Villasana –compilador de la edición– convocó a los narradores... Esta misma antología se publicará como e-book, término al que todavía no me acostumbro pero me llena de alegría al saber que circulará de web en web y miles de internautas disfrutarán más allá de las fronteras, algo tan necesario en los tiempos actuales cuando algunos se afanan por levantar muros y cerrar puertas."

Elena Poniatowska Amor

Six violent short stories from mexican authors: Alberto Chimal, Erika Mergruen, Yuri Herrera, Isaí Moreno, Úrsula Fuentesberain, Lorea Canales.

"Originality and the joy of writing abound in these stories, features that define each of these writers. Also present is violence, the thread that runs through each of these stories and serves as the watchword around which my friend Omar Villasana—the editor of this edition—has brought together each of these authors... This anthology will also be published as an e-book, a term to which I am still not accustomed but one that fills me with joy, knowing that it will circulate from web to web and that thousands of Internet users will be able to enjoy beyond the confines of physical borders, something so necessary in modern times when there are those who strive to build walls and close doors."

Elena Poniatowska Amor 田

No son tantas las estrellas/There Are Not So Many Stars

(Spanish/English).
Isaí Moreno (author).
Arthur M. Dixon (translator).
2019. 225 pages.
(Available in Kindle Format)
$18.00 usd
ISBN-13: 978-1732114463

El horror de la razón en el siglo de las luces, el palimpsesto de ese horror en el siglo del desencanto. Hay ocasiones en que la literatura logra mucho más que representar una época y aprehende la locura que le anima. No son tantas las estrellas (edición definitiva de Pisot) es la obra rara que sabe contar la historia de ciertos hombres en los que ha quedado la marca indeleble de tiempos monstruosos. Es por ello y por su escritura limpia y erudita, un libro destinado a convertirse en objeto de culto.

Yuri Herrera (Autor de los Trabajos del reino y Señales que precederán al fin del mundo) 囝

The horror of reason in the Age of Enlightenment, the palimpsest of that horror in the age of disenchantment. There are times when literature goes beyond representing an era and grasps the madness behind it. There Are Not So Many Stars (the definitive edition of Pisot) is that rare work that tells the story of certain men who bear the indelible mark of monstrous times. For this reason, and for its clean, erudite writing, this book is destined to become a cult object.

Yuri Herrera (author of Kingdom Cons and Signs Preceding the End of the World) 囝

KATAKANA FICTION

(fiction translated to english)

Unrepentant Times: Short stories by Mexican authors.

Omar Villasana (editor).
George Henson, Arthur M. Dixon,
Jose Armando Garcia, Silvia Guzman
(translators).
2018. 70 pages.
(Available in Kindle Format)
$10.00 usd
ISBN-13: 978-1732114418

Six short stories by Mexican authors: Alberto Chimal, Erika Mergruen, Yuri Herrera, Isaí Moreno, Úrsula Fuentesberain and Lorea Canales.

"Originality and the joy of writing abound in these stories, features that define each of these writers. Also present is violence, the thread that runs through each of these stories and serves as the watchword around which my friend Omar Villasana —the editor of this edition— has brought together each of these authors... This anthology will also be published as an e-book, a term to which I am still not accustomed but one that fills me with joy, knowing that it will circulate from web to web and that thousands of Internet users will be able to enjoy beyond the confines of physical borders, something so necessary in modern times when there are those who strive to build walls and close doors."

Elena Poniatowska Amor 冉

Immigration: The Contest (Bad News from The Island).

Carlos Gamez (author).
Arthur M. Dixon (translator).
2019. 132 pages.
(Available in Kindle Format)
$14.00 usd
ISBN-13: 978-1732114456

In a not-so-distant future, four immigrants will risk their lives in a "game" whose object is to reach the Promised Land once known as Europe. Carlos Gámez Pérez offers us this dystopian vision of a world that sometimes seems all too close to our own at a time when nationalisms are resurging around the globe. 🈳

The Most Fragile Objects.

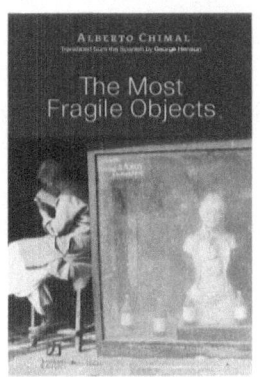

George Henson (translator).
2020. 126 pages.
(Available in Kindle format).
$12.00 usd
ISBN-13: 978-1732114494

The Most Fragile Objects, Chimal's first novel published in translation, tells three stories (maybe two, or just one) of people living secret lives in early 21st-century Mexico. They seem to indulge in wanton sex and power fantasies. But is everything what it appears to be? With a style that never resorts to titillation and a plot structure in which the factual and the dubious chase each other, The Most Fragile Objects, is an unusual, dark take on the themes of power, love, imagination, and freedom. ⊞

There Are Not So Many Stars
(definitive edition of Pisot)

Isai Moreno (author)
Arthur M. Dixon (translator)
2020. 114 pages
$12.00 usd
ISBN-13: 978-1734185010

The horror of reason in the Age of Enlightenment, the palimpsest of that horror in the age of disenchantment. There are times when literature goes beyond representing an era and grasps the madness behind it. There Are Not So Many Stars (the definitive edition of Pisot) is that rare work that tells the story of certain men who bear the indelible mark of monstrous times. For this reason, and for its clean, erudite writing, this book is destined to become a cult object.

Yuri Herrera (author of Kingdom Cons and Signs Preceding the End of the World) ⊞

COLECCIÓN PÉNDULO NAGARI
(Poesía en español)

miamimemata

Eduard Reboll 2017.
62 páginas.
$12.00 usd
ISBN-13: 978-1979104470

Poemas sutiles y propios. Localizados en el downtwon de Miami algunos. Fotografías y reflexiones urbanas que nos hablan del vivir aquí. Una observación casi antropológica del miamense de a pie. El mar y su ausencia, bajo el efecto lighthouse de Key Biscayne. E incluso, desde lo antagónico, hay una oda a la ciudad. Un cántico libre, una vez uno entiende como germina el día a día de los ciudadanos que la habitan en la bien llamada y querida Puerta de la Américas. ⌘

Aquí[Ellas] en Miami

Alejandra Ferrazza, Gloria Milá de la Roca
y Omar Villasana (editores).
2018. 126 páginas.
$16.00 usd
ISBN-13: 978-1732114432

Aquí[Ellas] en Miami está conformado por 24 poetas miamenses:
Lourdes Vázquez, Rosie Inguanzo, Mia Leonin, Kelly Martínez, Odalys
Interián, Martha Daza, Susana Biondini, Yosie Crespo, Lizette Espino-
sa, Glenda Galán, Teresa Cifuentes, Ana Kika, Judith Ghashghaie, Mar-
icel Mayor Marsán, Alejandra Ferrazza, Ximena Gómez, Ena Colum-
bié, Legna Rodríguez, María Juliana Villafañe, Gloria MiládelaRoca,
Pilar Vélez, Beatriz Mendoza, Lidia Elena Caraballo y Rubí Arana.
Aquí[Ellas] nos hablan sobre la nostalgia, el desamparo, el tiempo, el
vacío, también la esperanza, el amor y la libertad. Recurren a la historia, la familia, a recuerdos que las han marcado, llegando estos a ser
asideros vitales. La voz femenina se hace presente desde la visión
particular de cada una de ellas. Algunos poemas nos muestran una
cara de la ciudad que habitamos y que nos duele reconocer, mientras
que en otros nos relatan la belleza de los paisajes y sus calles. También surgen aquellos lugares que han quedado en la memoria y que
muchas veces quisieran volver a caminar. 卍

Malas noticias desde la isla

Carlos Gámez.
2018.
136 páginas.
(Disponible también en formato Kindle)
$14.00 usd
ISBN-13: 978-1732114425

En un futuro no muy lejano, cuatro inmigrantes arriesgarán su vida en un "juego" donde la apuesta es alcanzar la Tierra Prometida de lo que otrora se llamara Europa. Carlos Gámez Pérez nos entrega esta visión distópica, en un mundo que a ratos tristemente parece demasiado próximo, ante el resurgimiento de los nacionalismos a nivel global.

Miami Blue y otras historias

Xalbador García.
2019. 132 páginas.
(Disponible también en formato Kindle)
$10.00 usd
ISBN-13: 978-1732114487

En el mapa desconocido de Miami existe un universo habitado por parias, seres marginales que se confunden en el pantano de asfalto. Miami Blue y otras historias de Xalbador García nos ofrece la fotografía instantánea de esos seres (inmigrantes indocumentados, prostitutas, exiliados cubanos) que nos descubren la realización no del sueño, sino de la pesadilla americana.

Las noventa Habanas.

Dainerys Machado Vento

Dainerys Machado Vento
2019. 131 páginas
(Disponible también en formato Kindle)
$10.00 usd
ISBN-13: 978-1734185003

La Habana no es una sino muchas, cambia con la luz del día y las to-
nalidades del mar. En Las noventa Habanas, Dainerys Machado Vento, crea, desde la mirada femenina de lo cotidiano, recuerdos, esos
múltiples fragmentos que conforman el rompecabezas de la memoria, muestra, no una, sino múltiples ciudades con muros de agua,
donde la insatisfacción en un ambiente opresivo escapa a lo que de-
limita una extensión geográfica.

COLECCIÓN ENSAYO NAGARI

(Ensayo, reseña, cronica, varia en español)

Bajo la luz de mi lámpara de Ikea.

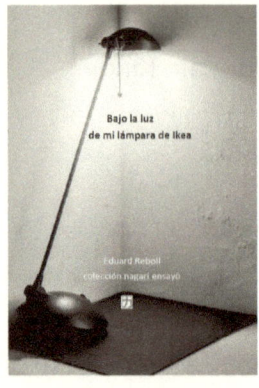

Eduard Reboll. 2018. 246 páginas.
$14.00 usd.
ISBN-13: 978-1732114401

Es bajo la luz de la lámpara retratada en la portada de este libro que nacen los textos que el lector está a punto de develar. Escritos que, desde el año 2013 fueron publicados en la columna mensual Bajo la luz de mi lámpara de Ikea en nagarimagazine.com versión online de la revista Nagari. Al presentar este libro, he pretendido como editor mostrar una estructura diferente a la experiencia cronológica que vivió el autor y, de alguna forma, encontrar el hilo que guio durante los últimos cinco años la creación literaria de sus artículos.

www.ingramcontent.com/pod-product-compliance
Lightning Source LLC
Chambersburg PA
CBHW021933170626
46807CB00007B/3080